MAXIMUM WARP

Book Two of Two

Dave Galanter and Greg Brodeur
Based upon STAR TREK and
STAR TREK: THE NEXT GENERATION
created by Gene Roddenberry.

D0386177

POCKET BOOKS
New York   London   Toronto   Sydney   Singapore

An *Original* Publication of POCKET BOOKS

POCKET BOOKS, a division of Simon & Schuster, Inc.
1230 Avenue of the Americas, New York, NY 10020

A VIACOM COMPANY

STAR TREK is a Registered Trademark of Paramount Pictures.

This book is published by Pocket Books, a division of Simon & Schuster, Inc., under exclusive license from Paramount Pictures.

ISBN: 0-671-04757-4

First Pocket Books printing March 2001

10 9 8 7 6 5 4 3 2 1

POCKET and colophon are registered trademarks of Simon & Schuster, Inc.

Printed in the U.S.A.

BOOK TWO

FOREVER DARK

Chapter One

U.S.S. Enterprise, NCC 1701-E
Klingon Empire
Lormit Sector

Three days ago

"GIVE ME ONE GOOD REASON why I shouldn't kill you, Picard."

He'd done it. Lotre had accomplished what so many had tried yet failed—he'd taken by force a Federation starship, and had its captain at his mercy.

The Klingon pulled his weapon away from the underside of Picard's chin and grabbed the captain around the neck with his open hand. Grunting, he strenuously lifted Picard off the deck of the bridge.

It was a moment to behold. Captain Jean-Luc Picard,

commander of the *Starship Enterprise,* relieved of his command—by this Romulan citizen. A Klingon who'd rejected his native culture, and done what no other Klingon ever had.

He couldn't help but glance around as the Starfleeters twitched in fear.

Lotre snickered. "Tell me why I shouldn't vaporize you this instant."

To his surprise, Picard was not gurgling his breaths through what should have been a collapsing trachea. Rather, Picard's posture was as if his feet were *not* dangling three inches over the deck.

"Because you can't," the Starfleet captain said in a perfectly even tone. His right hand came up and easily wrenched Lotre's fingers back painfully, awkwardly. The Klingon tried to pull away but the Terran's grip was too strong. Instead, Picard somehow gained footing on the deck. In one twisting motion he somehow managed to toss Lotre halfway across the bridge.

The lights seemed to wink out for a moment, but it was only Lotre's consciousness that flickered under the pain caused him. Anger overwhelmed the agony, however, and Lotre got back up on his feet. He waved off the others. They were needed to cover the rest of the bridge crew anyway. Picard was his alone.

He lunged, but with amazing speed Picard stepped out of the way and the Klingon slammed into the deck. He felt the Starfleeter lift him, punch his face, and let him drop to the deck again.

Lotre was dazed and bruised, and his lungs burned from what was probably a broken rib. He coughed up a spot of blood and looked up to see Picard standing over him ominously.

He seemed taller at this angle, stronger. And he wasn't even out of breath.

"Wha—what are you?" Lotre said with a gasp.

Picard smirked down at him. "Just a starship captain."

Lotre laughed painfully as he hooked his arm around Picard's legs and pulled him down to the deck, hard.

Recovering quickly, Picard cracked Lotre in the jaw with his boot. Lotre didn't shrink away, however—he looped his arm around Picard's extended leg, pulled the captain in, and drove the butt of his rifle unto Picard's gut.

In what seemed like a nanosecond, Picard was on his feet again. Lotre scrambled up as well, but a flurry of limbs—he wasn't sure if he was being kicked or hit—knocked him back to the deck.

In a red haze, Lotre's battle instinct took control. As Picard moved toward him again, Lotre fired his disruptor. The air on the bridge snapped with energy.

Captain Jean-Luc Picard clasped his hands over his ears and shrieked so loudly Lotre had to do the same. But then Picard folded in on himself, static electricity sparkling over his form as he disintegrated . . . and then was gone.

"I'm far too young to die," Picard said.

Spock looked up from his console. "I did try to delay it as long as possible. But given too many occurrences that are unlikely, they would soon deduce they're not in a natural environment."

5

Picard smiled slightly, despite the grave circumstances. "Ambassador, are you suggesting I can only defeat a Klingon in hand-to-hand combat on a holodeck where I reprogram my abilities?"

"Not at all, Captain." The Vulcan tabbed at his holodeck controls. "I suggest that is only the case with *this* Klingon."

Hesitating a moment, Picard nodded his good-natured acceptance of Spock's slight gibe. After all, part of the holodeck idea had been Spock's.

The captain watched Lotre on the screen a moment. What was within this man to fight so? Just a mercenary? That didn't seem to be the case. Why did he support the Romulan T'sart—a mass murderer who'd helped to kill thousands of other Klingons, and members of countless other races? Perhaps for the same reason Picard seemed to be helping T'sart—because the galaxy's well-being was at stake and the Romulan criminal might hold the key.

That didn't mean that Picard trusted T'sart. Both he and Spock thought the Romulan would attempt something—they just weren't sure what. But they'd found a virus in the data chip the Romulan had given them, and that alone was cause for concern. The virus has been programed to give T'sart computer access and to take down the shields at a specified time. Spock caught it before it infected the *Enterprise* computer core, but it was obvious T'sart wanted the shields out of the way for a reason.

Spock had suggested that if they could time it right, they could intercept the transporter beams of a boarding party. Picard agreed, and asked the Vulcan to set up a simulation on the holodeck. Beamed directly into a running program, the boarding party would think it was succeeding at taking over the *Enterprise,* and wouldn't call for reinforcements.

It was working, for now. But two questions remained: Who caused the explosions that *did* bring down the shields, and how?

T'sart had that answer and Picard wanted it. "Make sure Lotre and his team are occupied for now. Hide T'sart on their version of the ship. They'll be looking for him, and obviously we can't let them accomplish all their goals."

"Aye, sir." Spock nodded and went to work. He'd not been on active duty on a starship since before Picard was born, and yet he slipped back into it as if he'd never been away.

"Status on the enemy ship?"

"You were correct," Spock said, switching scanners. "They recloaked when our shields returned and they'd not heard from their comrades."

The captain cradled his chin in one hand. "They'll be back. Let's make sure we're ready for them." He began toward the turbolift.

"Where will you be?" Spock asked.

"Deck seven. I'm going to pay Mr. T'sart an overdue visit."

As Picard entered T'sart's cabin, he found the Romulan walking toward the doorway. "Captain, I believe I'm due in sickbay."

"You're going to be late." Picard laid one hand on

T'sart's arm and guided him back into the living quarters.

"Is something amiss?" T'sart asked. "I *did* notice you doubled my guard. And I thought I may have heard some explosions somewhere."

T'sart sat himself down into one of the more comfortable chairs and Picard remained standing.

"Surely you can be less obvious than that," Picard said coldly.

Adept at innocent-lamb expressions, T'sart smirked up at the captain. Picard wasn't impressed.

"You wound me, Captain."

Picard said, "The thought had crossed my mind."

As if some inner switch had been flipped, T'sart's expression changed instantly. He was serious now, and perhaps his lips were turned down with slight bitterness. "I assume Lotre has failed and is dead?"

Picard said nothing, preferring to let T'sart wonder about his comrade's fate.

T'sart shrugged. "I make no apologies, Captain. I don't trust you to do what needs to be done."

"You mean killing your own people," Picard barked.

"I have no 'people,'" T'sart said calmly as he leaned back into the easy chair. "I am an individual."

"Who sees himself as the *only* individual with rights, it would seem."

"Rights," T'sart scoffed. "A very Federation notion."

"I don't intend to debate philosophy with the likes of you," he said as he stepped toward the Romulan.

"Then why are you here?" T'sart's tone was annoyed, as if he didn't wish to be bothered with the frivolous lives and rights of others, and Picard felt as if he were talking to a petulant child.

"To give you an ultimatum. You will cooperate with us and cease your attempts to take over my ship."

T'sart sounded unimpressed. "Or?"

Picard put one hand on the back of T'sart's chair and spun the Romulan toward him so that they were almost nose to nose. "Or I continue on without you—and ask the Klingons to bring you back to Starbase 10."

"Leaving me in *their* 'care,' Picard?" T'sart didn't seem fazed by Picard's invasion into his personal space. Nothing fazed T'sart much, it seemed. "Doesn't that break your regulations? Leaving someone under your charge in such an . . . unhealthy situation?"

Picard pushed off T'sart chair and stood straight. "I can't contact Starfleet Command, and if you're right about the time this galaxy has left, there won't be a Starfleet to which I would need to answer. As for your well-being?" Picard let his lips curl into a slight snarl. "I'm relatively unconcerned about the repercussions of leaving you in the Klingons' hands."

"I see." For once, T'sart seemed speechless. Picard liked the idea of that.

"I'm glad we understand one another," the captain said. "Now, I'll have you escorted to sickbay."

T'sart stood slowly, his face contorted in a grimace. "I—"

He collapsed forward and Picard had to lunge forward to catch him before he hit the deck.

Supporting the Romulan in one arm, Picard awkwardly punched his combadge with the other. "Picard to sickbay. Medical emergency in T'sart's quarters!"

Damn. Not enough time.

"Saunders! Miketo! Get in here!"

"What happened?" Beverly Crusher pounced onto T'sart with a medical tricorder the instant his stretcher broke the sickbay threshold.

Picard helped the orderlies move the Romulan to the main biobed diagnostic table as the sickbay personnel came alive in a flurry of activity. "He collapsed."

"He's gone into respiratory arrest," Crusher said as she dropped the tricorder and scooped up a more sophisticated sensor. "Get that cart over here!"

Not wanting to be in the way, Picard stepped back. Here, on this table, was a man whom whole races would pay almost any price to see tortured and killed. Splayed across Dr. Crusher's biobed was someone who by most judgments didn't deserve to live—by dint of having killed so many.

And yet, the fate of the galaxy might truly be stored within him.

"It's as if there's fluid in his lungs, but there's not. Some sort of fibroid structures." Crusher was talking more to her staff than Picard, at least until she turned to him. "Was he coughing?"

The captain shook his head. "No, he was fine until he collapsed."

She slit T'sart's sleeve with a low-powered laser scissor and exposed his skin. "We're going to oxygenate and filter impurities out of his blood for now, but I'll need to operate to remove the tumors." She slapped some device on his arm and set about cutting open the front of his tunic. "Twenty-five cc's tri-ox, Romulan mixture."

"Is he going to live?" Picard asked.

Crusher didn't bother looking up. She was too intent on saving the life of a man everyone in the room probably hated. "I'll let you know."

Picard nodded. T'sart began to slacken under the drugs and the medical relief. He'd seen such a loose body posture many times before—in the bodies of the dead.

Chapter Two

**Private vessel *Loa-var*
Romulan space
Sector 36**

"I DON'T UNDERSTAND," TOBIN SAID, and Riker looked away for a moment. Those brown, penetrating eyes looked remarkably like those of a sad puppy, considering that he was a Romulan. Since the moment Riker, Deanna, and Data had beamed aboard to escape the notice of the Romulan fleet, not to mention their disintegrating shuttle, Riker had been avoiding Tobin's sad expression.

"I'm trying to explain . . ." he began, fidgeting with a circuit spanner as he tested a control board. ". . . well, see, what we need to do—"

Deanna stooped down and whispered. "I think he knows *what* you want to do, but not why."

"He does look more disappointed than confused, sir," Data whispered, peeking his head from behind an access alcove in just to the door of Tobin's small engine room.

"A little help, here, people?" Riker grumbled back at them. He then turned fully to Tobin, who sat slumped against the bulkhead opposite them. "Tobin, do you understand what's at stake here?"

"I suppose I don't," the Romulan said matter-of-factly, his brows knitting together in befuddlement.

Deanna had been standing next to Riker, configuring the panel over his head, but now she moved closer to Tobin and sat herself down next to him. "You know about the dead zones, right?" she asked softly.

"Power deserts," he said. "Yes. I have not seen any myself, but everyone knows of the problems with subspace communications and the lost ships. SLANN blames the Federation, in fact, but trading ships have leaked that even the Federation has these problems."

"SLANN?" Riker asked.

Data once again dipped his head into the room. "The Romulan Empire's government news service, sir."

Riker nodded. *Of course.*

"We're trying to stop those power deserts," Deanna told him.

"And . . . so you must use my ship?" Tobin nodded and as if that settled it, albeit sadly, and picked up the plasma conduit he'd been repairing.

"You want to come to the Federation, right?" Riker asked, selling the incentive with a wide grin.

"Of course I want to get to the Federation," Tobin said. "It is why I have the cloaked ship."

"You did not have to sneak in," Data offered innocently, pulling himself out of the alcove and closing its hatch. "The Federation will grant citizenship to all eligible individuals."

Tobin smiled, good-naturedly if just a touch condescendingly. "I was not attempting to sneak into the Federation, I was attempting to sneak out of the empire."

Data nodded. "Ah."

Hiding their faces a bit, Deanna and Riker both stifled grins.

"This is our situation, Tobin," Riker finally was able to begin again. "There is a phenomena, this dead zone problem. The source of it somewhere in Romulan space—"

"It is? Where?"

Riker sighed. "Somewhere. The point . . ." He looked back toward the Romulan. ". . . is that we need to travel through Romulan space to get there—"

"I will take you—" Tobin offered.

"No, not just us. Our entire ship."

The Romulan's eyes grew wide. "A Federation starship?"

"Yes—"

He seemed fascinated. "Which one?"

Riker hesitated a moment, then decided it couldn't hurt to tell him. *"Enterprise."*

"You're from *Enterprise?"* Tobin stood excitedly, causing Riker and Troi to rise as well.

Unsure if this was favorable to their situation or not, Riker asked slowly, "Is . . . that good?"

"It's amazing!" Tobin said excitedly.

Riker looked over to Deanna. "Is 'amazing' good?"

"It feels like it's good," she offered.

"*Enterprise* is well known," Tobin said. He was bouncing on the balls of his feet now. "Famous even in the empire."

"That can't be good." Riker frowned.

"Oh, yes, it is good. Well, not to many, but to me it is." Tobin shook a finger and grinned knowingly. "I hear things. About the Federation, about Starfleet." The Romulan's good nature was a bit infectious. No wonder Deanna was smiling so much. Despite their grave mission, Riker couldn't help but smile a bit himself.

"What kind of things?" Data asked.

"Data, we're getting off topic." Riker motioned an end to that line of questioning and waved to get the Romulan's attention away from Data. "Mr. Tobin, we can make these dead zones go away—"

"Or at least make sure no new ones develop," Deanna said, and Riker glared at her a moment. He was becoming very tried of being interrupted.

"*But,*" he emphasized, "we'll need to bring our starship across Romulan space."

"And you want me to bring you back to your starship?" Tobin asked. "I can do that. May I go with you after that? To the Federation?"

"No—" Riker tried to explain what he really needed.

"I may not come with you?" Angled with deep disappointment, Tobin's features seemed to crumple inward.

"No, not that," Riker snapped, then sighed. "Please stop interrupting."

"I'm sorry," the Romulan said despondently.

"You can come to the Federation." Riker put his arm

around Tobin's shoulder and guided him toward the doorway. He felt like he was having a conversation with a young cadet. "We'll make sure that happens. *If* we survive. But . . ." He sighed. "I've forgotten where I was."

"We need to get the *Enterprise* across Romulan space," Tobin reminded him.

"Right. Thanks. We need to help our ship cross Romulan space undetected."

Tobin shook his head and pursed his lips a moment before speaking. "I do not think my cloak would work in your ship's systems."

"We don't need the cloak. Just an element used to catalyze Romulan plasma exhaust. Barantium. That's why we were going to that subspace relay station. Apparently it had a docking port with supplies so a vessel could make emergency repairs."

The Romulan nodded solemnly and Riker figured it was making sense. At least to someone.

"I see," he said. "This relay station exploded? That was the energy wave on my sensors right before you beamed onto my ship, yes?"

"Yes. Now we need to find another source of barantium. We need your help with that. And you just happen to have a ship that can carry more than we need." Riker smiled. Finally he'd been able to get out more than one sentence before being interrupted.

Tobin hesitated, but only as he considered it. Slowly he positively accepted the idea. "I—I suppose I can help. Will this be dangerous?"

"Probably," Deanna said softly as they all stepped onto his compact bridge.

"Hmmmm..." The Romulan calmly deliberated with himself.

"Hey, you want to earn passage, right?" Riker asked, flashing his smile again.

"This is his ship, sir."

"Quiet, Mr. Data."

"Yes, sir."

"Do you know where we can get some barantium?" Riker asked as Tobin lowered himself into his combination helm/command chair.

"I'm not sure," Tobin replied. "I know of a few places where ships are repaired. Non-military repair facilities. I assume you don't want to visit a military one."

"No, we don't."

Tobin nodded.

"It would also have to be something out of the way—somewhere where requesting a lot of this material wouldn't be noticed," Riker told him.

"How much do you need?"

Riker looked up to Data and let him answer. "Half a kiloton."

"That would be noticed everywhere," Tobin said somberly.

All of them frowned.

"But," the Romulan added more cheerfully, "some would overlook it, if properly bribed."

"Where?" Riker grinned.

"Lantig. A planetoid. Not too distant, but off most of the trade routes. There is a repair facility there. Sometimes the administrator will trade for supplies. It is not a well-kept facility or a very technological port, but nonetheless he will be suspicious that we are not in need of repair."

Riker stood and patted Tobin on the shoulder. "Then, we'll have to be."

"I do not under—" Tobin stood and followed Riker as he walked toward the door back to the main deck. "No, please—"

"Sorry, Mr. Tobin," Riker said.

"But, we just finished repairing the ship from the last time you broke it."

Commander Riker turned back toward his crew-mates. "Mr. Data . . . some simple sabotage, please. Not debilitating, but in obvious need of repair."

"Aye, sir." Data picked up a tool kit he'd recently set down and followed Riker toward the engines.

"But—" Tobin sputtered after him then turned to Deanna. "But . . ."

She shrugged. "What else can we do?"

And as she left too, Tobin found himself alone on his small bridge.

"But . . . I have nothing with which we can barter."

Chapter Three

"YOU ONLY HAVE THE ONE transporter pad?" Riker quickly ducked his head in and out of the single transporter alcove. It was dingy and didn't look well maintained, and Riker probably had the same facial expression he had when eating at a restaurant with dirty glasses. "This is it?"

"Yes," Tobin said, checking the power cells to the unit. "I never thought I would need more."

Riker frowned and looked over Tobin's shoulder at the control panel. "It's a little old. What's the transfer rate?"

"Seventeen point three seconds at ten thousand kilometers."

Old and slow, Riker thought. "It'll have to do."

Data stepped into the small transporter room through the only door. "Sir, perhaps I should go in your place."

Patting him on the shoulder, Riker smiled. "Data, you're an excellent second officer, you play a mean hand of poker, and you have the nicest cat in all of Starfleet. But, while outwardly you could pass as an alien, all they'd need to do is scan you to see you're an android."

Tobin spun around, eyes wide with awe. "He *is?*"

"Yes, sir," Data replied matter-of-factly.

Tentatively, Tobin reached out one hand and felt Data's arm. "I couldn't tell at all," he breathed. "Simply amazing. Who built you?"

"We made him from a kit," Riker said before Data could reply in great depth. "Come on, we don't have time for this."

Marching up the main corridor of Tobin's vessel, Riker gave Data some final orders. Tobin followed closely behind.

"Now, if the repair technicians make any wide-scans, you'll be masking your bio and power signatures, right?"

"Yes, sir."

"How well were you able to hide Tobin's cloaking device?"

"Somewhat. It looks like a large power conduit now."

Riker stopped and turned toward the android. "Won't that seem suspicious?"

Data seemed to consider that a moment. "Less suspicious than before, sir."

With a sigh, Riker continued up the hallway and Data followed.

They joined Deanna on the hauler's bridge. While Riker was talking to Data, Tobin had retrieved some sort of small case.

"Here, I've brought you the proper garb," he said.

Smiling pleasantly, Deanna took the case. Deanna's smiles were infections and both Riker and Tobin found themselves reciprocating. Perhaps feeling left out, Data smiled as well. Data's smiles had improved greatly since he installed his emotion chip, but Riker still thought he looked a bit goofy.

"A bit drab, isn't it?" Deanna said as she pulled the dark gray material from the bag.

Tobin shrugged. "Indentured servants don't wear garish attire."

Running his hand through what looked like a tunic and trousers, Riker asked, "This looks like mine."

"It is," Tobin said.

"Yes. Female indentured servants—"

"Slaves," Deanna interrupted.

Unwilling to have this debate again, Tobin half shrugged and half nodded. Deanna had spent some time posing as a Tal Shiar agent aboard a Romulan warbird, so she'd gotten a crash course in several Romulan cultural mores. As far as she was concerned, this was slavery, not servitude.

"In any case," Tobin said, "Female indentured servants wear these clothes."

Examining the form-fitting robe that Tobin handed him, Riker scowled.

"I meant no offense. But these are the accoutrements one of her status would wear." Tobin cast his head downward and looked as if he was trying to explain to Riker how he'd accidentally killed the family dog. "If you do not wish to attract undue attention . . ."

"I thought we were both slaves," Riker said.

"Indentured servants," Tobin corrected. "And you must realize, the purpose of such laborers is not for their brute strength." He cleared his throat, looked away, then back, then to Deanna—but not her face— and then his gaze *finally* settled back on Riker.

Riker pulled in a deep breath and pushed it out strongly. "You're sure you don't have anything we could trade for the barantium?"

The Romulan shrugged and shook his head. "My vessel is all I have."

"Fine. Let's get this over with then," Riker said. "Data, keep a transporter lock on us at all times."

"This equipment does not have that feature, sir," Data said, showing Riker a screen on one of the small consoles. "But I will keep scanning for human and Betazoid life-forms."

Nodding his grudging acceptance, Riker moved toward the doorway. "Today seems to be a 'take-what-you-can-get' kind of day."

Lantig Marketplace
Romulan space
Sector 37

The sun beat down on them as they walked from the repair facility administrator's center to the market, but it wasn't a warming sun. The temperature was probably between eight and ten degrees Celsius and so as they trudged across the dusty square, the sun seemed to give more light than heat.

It was a rural planet, scantily populated, too far off the beaten Romulan path to be of military value. That explained why the security force seemed mostly administrative. They probably arrested drunks, took bribes, and led lives of dull desperation. The city they'd beamed down to looked like every picture Riker had ever seen of old railroad towns on Earth—where when the work was done the village was abandoned and forgotten. Surely no one truly called this place home.

"I urge you to be obedient and passive," Tobin whispered to them, despite not a soul being on the streets, let alone within earshot. "The petitioners in this market will not appreciate forceful servants."

"Slaves," Deanna said somewhat indignantly.

Riker smiled. She had her principles, always, and wasn't afraid to let them be known.

"In the empire, *most* are slaves to the state," Tobin said.

"Not the 'petitioners,' I assume," she responded.

"The petitioners are those who, well they don't *own* land—no one really owns land in the empire—but they are allowed to lease it from the state at a percentage of what they may earn."

"From farming?" Riker asked.

Tobin shrugged and Riker realized it was a motion the Romulan made quite often. "Farming, energy production, manufacturing, what have you."

"Okay," Riker began, "let's say we remain sold today. We wouldn't be working in those areas, right?"

"No." Tobin paused as he tripped on a loose stone in the pavement and Riker caught him. He whispered a thank-you, and then continued. "Such things are highly automated, of course."

From the corner of his eye, Riker saw someone in a window across the way watching them. So did Tobin, who hit Riker with the back of his hand as soon as he did. "Never touch me again. Never!" Tobin yelled.

Surprised more at Tobin's sudden change in attitude than actually being struck, it took Riker half a second to flinch and affix an appropriately contrite expression on his face.

"I will explain you don't speak the local language," Tobin said quietly. "Be sure not to react to anything people might say." They were both wearing inner-ear translators so they could follow what was happening. "And do not take offense when I hit you again."

"Again?" Riker stopped and looked at him.

Tobin had to stop, hit him again, and Riker reacted a bit faster this time with a flinch.

"This is because I disabled your ship before, right?"

"It is expected, to show your obedience," Tobin said. "Deanna will hit you as well."

Riker smirked. "Oh, she will, will she?"

"You are male," the Romulan said matter-of-factly. "The female servants have standing and authority."

The *Enterprise* first officer sighed. "This day just keeps getting better."

Shivering, Deanna nuzzled against Riker playfully. "You've never had a problem with females in authority before."

"I've never been sold before." Riker hugged her with the arm that cradled her.

"Silence now," Tobin said as he took Riker and Deanna inside and motioned for them to sit and wait for him. As they did, Riker couldn't help but imagine what it must be like for people to really come here and sign away their lives. No bars, no chains, no cages, but they made themselves slaves nevertheless. It was a dismal planet, and if an asteroid wiped it out of existence, he wondered how many would care. It was, in fact, a dead zone in itself.

Tobin had walked up to someone behind a counter and was talking with them. He filled out some forms, signing with a retina scan, and after a little more discussion he motioned for Riker and Deanna to join him.

When they had, Tobin nodded them through another door and, once inside the inner area, Riker saw that there were several such "servants," all clad similarly, and of a variety of races. No one was chained or looked to be there against their wills. Of course, most Romulans were not in chains, yet could not choose to leave Romulan space without permission.

Riker had stopped and Tobin urged him along with a thwack to the back of his head. He forced himself not to frown, but he was sure Deanna felt his displeasure. If only because she giggled again in his mind.

After only a few steps he stopped to glare at her and so she also slapped him, hard, against the back. He flinched and moved on, but didn't remove his glare.

"Stop being disobediant," Tobin whispered to them.

A large Romulan in elaborately colored robes approached. "What have we here?"

"Two humanoids," Tobin said, smiling. "I believe they are from the Lornakan system."

"Are you selling separately?" the fat Romulan asked.

With a glint in his eye that to Riker seemed a bit too enthusiastic, Tobin smiled wider. "That would depend on how much you're paying."

"I have no use for this one," the man said of Riker as he waved the Starfleet officer away.

Tobin pushed Riker and Deanna back together. "But I have need to sell both."

The buyer frowned.

"But," Tobin quickly added, *"if* I get a good enough price for them respectively . . ."

Riker didn't like the idea of them being sold to different buyers. How would he protect her? Or, since she had more experience with Romulans, how would she protect him?

Again they spoke to one another without words.

I'll be fine, she told him.

The fat man was sizing Deanna up, and Riker didn't like just how intently he was doing so.

This guy already thinks he owns you, he thought to her.

Keep your chivelry in check, I know what I'm doing.

He *knows what he's doing too,* Riker thought. *And that's the part that worries me.*

"I don't like this." Riker told Tobin as they watched Deanna walk off with her buyer.

Her buyer, he thought, and smothered a sigh.

"It was a good price for her," Tobin assured him as he guided them toward some other shoppers.

"Is that supposed to make me feel better?"

The entire situation was ridiculous. They were selling themselves into Romulan slavery to gather enough money to buy what they needed to fulfill their mission and bribe the proper Romulan authorities. Surely there was another way.

Okay, he had to admit, this hadn't bothered him until he saw Deanna's buyer.

Tobin said, "I was not attempting to lift your spirits with my comment, except to point out that we are working toward *your* goal. This is not my mission. I am only trying to help. In truth, we received a good price for her. If we can get half that amount for you we'll have enough to purchase your barantium and bribe the administrator, if he isn't too greedy."

Riker knew that Tobin was absolutely right. And Picard—and their mission—was depending on him. "Why did he hustle Deanna out of here so quickly?"

"There are many regulations," Tobin said. "Many agreements they must sign. They have been taken to speak with a government bureaucrat about all of that."

Riker shuffled forward in the moccasin-like loafers he'd been given. He hated them, and rest of the servant's garb, and longed for his uniform. "Great. More bureaucrats."

"It *is* what we have most of in our system." Tobin motioned toward a group of Romulans who seemed to be looking their way. "Now we must find a buyer for you."

Before them were a few people of various ages, talking with one another about something Riker couldn't quite hear. Only one stood out from the group. She was dressed in bright robes, where the others were not, and while seemingly rather old, she walked quickly and it seemed her eyes were very alive. She noticed Riker looking, and so she smiled. For some reason, that made him nervous.

Others also looked, but after staring at Riker and Tobin quite a while, she finally walked toward them.

"Hello."

"Greetings, good lady." Tobin bowed. "Are you looking for a manservant?"

"I am," she replied, and dipped her head back to him as a show of mutual respect. "What are this one's skills?"

Tobin smiled. "Oh, wide and various, I assure you."

The old woman looked deeply into Riker's eyes for a moment. He couldn't help but be pulled into her eyes a bit as well. He liked her. Damn it all, she might buy him.

"Can you cook?" she asked.

"Oh, he does not speak a familiar tongue, and I am without a Universal Translator," Tobin said, trying to draw her attention away from Riker's face. "My name is Potaar . . . and you are?"

She turned and answered him "Nien Ch'lin. A pleasure to meet you, Potaar."

Tobin nodded and smiled politely.

"I am looking for a skilled servant. If I cannot interview him myself I will need to know how to contact you should he not be satisfactory."

"Of course." He offered his hand and she placed a padd into it. With a few quick dabs he entered what Riker assumed was a false address.

"What price are you asking?" Nien asked.

Tobin told her and she shook her head. "That is too high." She turned and began to walk away.

"Wait!" Tobin called after her and took a step forward. "We could—discuss it."

Nien turned back with grace and composure. "I mean no disrespect to you, sir, but you are selling the services of a man whom I may not even interview. I have but your word for his skills, and the price you ask is too high."

A strong woman, and noble in her way. She reminded Riker of one of his aunts. He remembered when he was young he'd always thought his aunt rather cold and stodgy—she'd had so many rules and was not easy on a boy without a mother, and, for all intents and purposes, without a father—but when Riker had returned from the Academy, she was the most proud of any of his mother's sisters. She'd told him she respected him so much, and always had. That was what he'd taken as stodgy—her formal respect for him.

Nien had that . . . formality that was not from pomposity, but honor.

Tobin had it as well. "Our price, as I indicated, is somewhat negotiable, of course."

Looking down at her padd, Nien keyed in an amount. By the looks of her credits balance, it was most of what she had.

"I can pay this." She showed Tobin the figure.

Tobin saw the amount and typed a revision into Nien's padd. "I can accept no lower than this."

Two honest people, making a fair bargain for the life of another. *What a galaxy,* Riker thought.

After some thought Nien nodded. "Very well," she said, and Riker had been sold.

* * *

Nien's estate was large and empty of people and yet it felt more like a home than a showpiece. She did not have great statuary or expensive works of art; rather, the walls were cluttered with pictures of her family. Riker assumed the furniture, older but well kept, was also family heirlooms. It looked antique: carved woods he'd never seen, thick varnish worn in the most used areas. Yes, her house even reminded Riker of his aunt's.

As they sat in what he would have considered a living room, Nien made a motion that suggested he should speak. Of course: the Universal Translator would need to hear him before it could know into what language her Romulan dialect should be interpreted.

He debated playing dumb, but doing so would only delay the inevitable and might actually be a problem if she decided to return him to Tobin, based on his refusal to speak.

"Hello," he said finally, knowing that one word was probably enough. Most Universal Translators tried the most used languages first.

"Hello," she replied. The one word had done the trick.

She paused as if she might say more, but was silent instead. It seemed she felt somewhat awkward about whatever was to come. Riker felt the same. So far this had not been what he expected at all.

"What is your name?" she asked finally.

"Riker."

"R'ker," she tried to repeat.

He corrected her. "Riker."

"Ri-ker."

He shrugged. "Sure."

"I am pleased to meet you, Ri-ker," she said, folding her hands on her lap. "Do you cook?"

"Some."

Nien nodded and seemed to be looking for other things she might ask. For someone who wanted so badly to interview him just an hour before she didn't have much to say. After another few minutes she finally asked, "Do you have any skills in systems maintenance? Computer programming?"

"A little of that too."

She smiled. "A little? Are there any skills in which you actually excel?"

Trying to remain noncommittal, Riker shrugged again. "I can fly a shuttle, fix things. Basic repair."

Not quite sighing, perhaps just breathing in and out thoughtfully, Nien shifted in her seat. "I see. There are servants' quarters south of the main house, but they've gone unused for some years. Perhaps later you can repair them for yourself. Expand them into a home."

Riker stared at her for a while. He couldn't deny liking this woman's poise and grace. She'd given a good deal of her savings to purchase his services and she talked of his long-term stay. Why wouldn't she? She bought into a ten-year deal.

And he knew he wouldn't even be with her the whole day. Suddenly what began as a righteous plan was seeming more seedy. "If that's what you want," he told her softly.

"I do not have a great deal of money," she told him as she began to rise. "A pension from my husband is all. But we can trade a bit for any materials you need."

Riker sighed. She wasn't going to make this easy. Who knew that the Romulan's nastiest secret weapon would be guilt.

He rose with her, not simply out of respect, but to help her stand as he allowed her to brace herself on him. "Understood."

Noticing his sour expression, Nien took his arm as they walked toward another room. "Please, do not be dismayed. I know people don't usually enter into these agreements because they've met with good fortune, but I believe this will work out." She patted the back of his hand. "If you are kind and loyal, I shall be as well."

"You're already very kind, that I can see," Riker said.

Nien laughed. "I am an old woman and you would be foolish to try and court me, young man."

Now they both laughed, and Riker wasn't feigning his delight at all.

In the few hours that followed, Nien gave Riker a small tour of the estate. Some of this was on foot, but most was in one room with a large monitor where sensor cameras showed him the extent of all the once-grand home had to offer.

It was becoming late in the afternoon and Nien began to look somewhat tired. She escorted Riker to the kitchen and showed him where cooking utensils and foodstuffs were kept.

He nodded, and after she left him alone, he sat in one of the kitchen chairs and wondered what in hell he was doing here. He knew the logistics and their plan—he just didn't think he'd end up having such a pleasant day with the person who bought him. Why couldn't she be rude and obnoxious, and deserving of being robbed blind, like the guy who bought Deanna?

Okay, that was a bad thing to think about. Now he was feeling guilty *and* worried. What was taking Tobin so long? What if he took the money and ran? No— Riker didn't think both he *and* Deanna were that bad at judging character. Especially Deanna.

After a few minutes he set about trying to make dinner.

Riker loved to cook and he fancied himself a not-half-bad chef—at least for those meals he knew how to prepare. While all Starfleet ships, and most Federation homes, had replicators, food was still grown. Despite most people being unable to really taste the difference, many suggested that naturally grown and handmade food was still the best.

The only problem here was that he didn't recognize most of the foods. He didn't read Romulan, and so labels on jars didn't help. But he did find some things that were obviously eggs, and he only hoped they scrambled like Terran chicken eggs.

There was something on the kitchen counter that looked like a potato but tasted like corn—interesting, to say the least. So, he took it, diced that and a few other vegetables that tasted fine, and put them into two omelettes.

From the refrigerator he found some kind of juice and something with a soupy texture that tasted like a sharp cheese.

He swilled the cheesy sauce over the omelettes and declared them finished.

Ready to serve, he brought Nien's plate into the dining room to find that she'd set two places at the table.

She noticed he had her plate only. "I don't expect you to eat alone," she said. "And I hope you don't expect me to."

Riker smiled. "No, ma'am."

She sat and he put her plate before her, and then he went to get his own. As he lowered himself to the table she said, "Well, whatever it is, it certainly smells good."

"Thank you. I really don't know much about the kind of food these are, I just—"

Nien lowered her head close to the omelette and sniffed. "Yes, I—I've never quite seen these foods together in such a manner."

To his surprise, Riker was a bit nervous. How good it tasted really didn't matter—he'd be gone soon and . . . well, he wanted it to taste good to her anyway.

Before Nien had a chance to taste hers, Riker took a bite himself and, while it wasn't the best he'd eaten, it certainly wasn't horrible. A little tangy for his tastes, but nothing inedible.

Tentatively, Nien dabbed her fork into the omelette and brought some to her lips. She was very polite, but Riker had seen an expression like hers before. Come to think of it, he'd seen the same expression on Deanna the first time he'd cooked for her.

"You don't like it."

Nien was very quick to shake her head. "No, it's very . . . good. Exotic."

He squinted in a partial wince. "I've mixed foods one wouldn't normally mix, haven't I?"

She didn't quite nod, but as she dabbed her lips with a napkin she made a motion with her head that was mostly affirmative. "Well, it's an interesting . . . experiment. Nothing wrong with a little change of pace." As if suddenly an aftertaste exerted itself she looked around, eyes open widely. "Is there anything to drink?"

He immediately poured her some juice and she promptly gulped it down. When she'd finished, she sat back in her chair and smiled up at him ruefully. "I can see I'll have to teach someone how to cook."

Riker frowned, not so much because he'd made her a bad meal but because she had no idea he'd never get the chance again. He wasn't wearing a timepiece, but his internal clock told him that soon he'd be beamed up, and Deanna as well wherever she was, and they'd both leave this planet forever, never to return.

And Nien would be without what she'd purchased. While the system which allowed such slaves might be corrupt, she was certainly not, and all she was trying to do was survive.

"What's wrong?" she asked him. "Please don't feel bad that I didn't finish. My age . . . I'm just not used to the more spicy meals, that's all."

He lowered his gaze. "No, it's not that."

She looked at him a long time, and he wasn't sure what else to say.

Finally, when she spoke again, it was in English, and without a translator. "You're not who you say, are you?"

Chapter Four

Romulan Warbird *Makluan*
Klingon space
Malinga Sector

SUB-COMMANDER FOLAN HAD BEEN WATCHING Medric's movements among the crew. He'd spent a lot of time on a lot of decks, mingling with too many crewman with whom he'd not usually have lowered himself to speak.

As she sat in her quarters—a cabin that had too recently been Commander J'emery's—Folan felt very alone.

There had always been things she could cling to: her career, her status, her duties. Now those were gone, and while her status was the highest it could now be on the *Makluan,* that was no position of camaraderie. She felt trapped in the capacity as the person in command—unable to get out once inside—much like the power deserts that now peppered all of space.

She shouldn't be here, she thought. She should be on the bridge. But she'd been there since this all began and was exhausted by the events, mentally as well as physically. If Folan didn't try to get some rest she would surely make a mistake that would mean her own death, as well as the death of her mission.

Her "mission." Her jihad, really. She seethed with hate, at T'sart, at Picard . . . but she wasn't getting any rest this way. Forcing herself away from the desk, she first thought about lying on the bed and attempting actual sleep. But in midstride toward the bunk-berth, she stopped and decided she should probably have an active response to Medric's meddling with the crew. If he was going to talk among them and persuade them, why couldn't she?

No, she thought, hesitating again before she reached the door, that was rational-scientist thought. She had to think like a soldier. She should confront Medric.

Yes, and be backed up by security.

No! Not security. She should go alone.

Yes, that would look stronger.

No, wait. That would be stupid. She should do none of those things. She should confront him on the bridge with witnesses, both to protect her from him and witness her bravery before him.

Folan sighed. She was making too much of this, thinking too much—again, the scientist. Well, more the schoolgirl really. *Make a decision,* she told herself, *and stick with it.*

She nodded to herself and stepped out into the corridor.

A crewman was marching toward her from the left. He was looking intently at her, oddly so, and it sent a shudder down her spine. Instinctively she began to turn the other way. That was when she stopped. A different crewman was treading toward her from that direction.

Folan almost stopped and ducked back into her quarters but thought she might have a better chance on the move. If she could get past them, run for the turbolift . . .

They obviously sensed her change in body language—if not her fear—because both men quickened their pace.

She was weaponless, and that had been a foolish mistake. She wasn't used to needing a weapon simply to walk the decks of her own vessel, but obviously she did. Probably thanks to Medric.

Not completely helpless, Folan leapt into the man closest to her and they both went tumbling. Since she was the one who knew they'd both be down, she was the first to recover. Rolling shoulder to knees, she was on her feet fast and ahead of the one man left standing—he'd had to dodge around his downed partner.

Adrenaline now on her side, Folan plunged away from them and up the corridor. But not all the way up. Just far enough to catch her breath. She might not have had a disruptor, but she had a ceremonial knife. Maybe she'd not practiced with it in years, but she *had* been trained. Now was the time to see just how well.

The blade unsheathed awkwardly and so she wasn't off to a good start.

Both pursuers were on their feet now and they smirked at her ungraceful bearing.

"You're going to stand here and fight us both?" the one on the left asked.

He was closer.

Slowly, Folan shook her head and eyed the disruptor the closer one had pulled from his tunic.

"It's over," he said.

She ran—around the corner and just beyond it, where she stopped short. He followed and as he rushed around toward her, she rammed her dagger into his chest with one hand, and took his weapon with her other. His already weakening carcass dropped to the deck.

Moving the disruptor to her right hand she felt blood—her attacker's—already becoming sticky in her palm. She moved quickly up the corridor, turned, and extended her arm.

Folan held the weapon threateningly at the last assailant as the man shoved his comrade's fallen body out of his way. Not yet dead, the injured man grunted as he rolled, then stopped with a thud.

The standing one snarled and kicked the disruptor out of her hand as he pulled out his own in one flowing motion.

"You insufferable . . ." He backhanded her in the jaw with his weapon hand. She fell against the bulkhead and slid down to the deck. Just a few feet from her, the man she'd stabbed lay gurgling his last breathes. Surely, she thought as she tasted blood in her mouth, she would be next.

The man took a step toward her, aiming his weapon. "You are relieved of your command," he said.

Folan closed her eyes and waited for that death. She couldn't outrun the weapon and she could no longer fight. The blow to her jaw had her a bit dazed and in her darkness she wondered when he would finally do the deed and pull the trigger. He was probably watching her cower—taking pleasure in her humiliation.

Not wanting to give him any more of that satisfaction, she opened her eyes . . . just as a disruptor whine split the air, and her attacker vaporized.

Up the corridor, Medric stood over the other crewman's body—the one she'd stabbed and who lay dying. Medric aimed, fired, and the last of Folan's assailants was also gone in a haze of bio-dust that settled to the deck in an electrical puff.

Folan looked up in surprise. *"Y-you* saved me?"

"Of course," Medric said as he reached down toward her with his open hand.

She stared as if it had fifteen fingers.

"Why?" She didn't take the hand; rather, she just sat against the bulkhead and continued to study it. "You need me," she said finally as he took her arm and hoisted her up. Finally she stood on her own.

Medric nodded. "In a way, yes."

"But you don't like me." It wasn't a question, just a statement, and from the way she said it she thought her lip must be swollen.

"I don't like anyone," he told her. "You're nothing special in that respect." He motioned up the corridor toward her cabin.

She didn't move. "Yesterday you looked as if you would've liked to see me dead yourself."

Again he gestured up the corridor. "I'd like to see everyone dead. You're nothing special in that respect either."

"Charming," she said dryly, and this time she began walking with him. "So why save me if you wouldn't mind seeing me dead?"

"As you said—I need you."

She glared at him sideways. "For?"

When he spoke his tone was quieter than usual. Not softer, just more secretive. "I need you to continue on your course. I need you to run this ship for me."

"For you?"

"For me." He stopped and nodded toward her cabin door, silently suggesting they enter.

Folan looked at him very suspiciously.

He sighed. "I'm not interested in you sexually, I assure you."

She paused, considered that, and though she wasn't sure if she wanted to be relieved or insulted, she nevertheless decided it was likely the truth. She let him follow her in.

"What do you mean run this ship for you? You're just a centurion," she said.

He moved to her desk and sat behind it nonchalantly. "I'm Tal Shiar."

Folan kept herself from stumbling back into the other chair. She did fall into it a bit more than was comfortable and she noticed a headache forming behind her eyes. She wondered if she might have a slight concussion. Perhaps she was delirious. Tal Shiar? Medric? *Tal Shiar?*

"You—you're telling me that, and . . . are you sure I'm not about to die?"

"Not if I can help it." Medric's smile was odd. Perhaps because he was Medric and Folan had rarely seen him smile, but more likely it was because a Tal Shiar was smiling and, well, the whole idea was bizarre.

"Why?" she asked. "Why would you want to save me? Why not kill me and take over this ship yourself?"

"Don't think I didn't consider that. But I tested you, and you have the drive to do this. And I've talked with the crew, and at least half of them support you." He leaned back, relaxed. "And, before T'sart sabotaged your experiment, we expected it to succeed."

" 'We' being the Tal Shiar?"

"Of course."

"And then . . ." She looked up confused. "When were you planning to kill me?"

"We were planning to offer you membership."

"In the Tal Shiar."

"No, the Senate," he snapped sarcastically. "Of course the Tal Shiar!"

Still, she didn't understand. "Why?"

"Because you have a brilliant scientific mind," Medric said. "And we can use you."

"But you can't use T'sart?"

"T'sart," Medric hissed his name, "was offered membership long ago. He turned it down."

This was all too much to take. Folan was feeling dizzy . . . and yet, also exhilarated. The power she could have as a member of the Tal Shiar . . . yes, their standards were rigorous, but they would become the only standards she need conform to. "Has that ever happened? Someone refusing to join?"

Medric's expression was sour. "A handful of individuals who came to regret their misstep. As will T'sart."

"And I'll do that for you?"

"You'll make sure he pays for his treachery," Medric said. "And you'll have accomplished your first Tal Shiar mission with honor."

Much to consider, Folan thought. And she wondered—how much more did Medric, as a Tal Shiar, know about the entire situation?

"Is Picard part of it?" she asked.

"T'sart is on *Enterprise*," he said. "What do you think?"

"I'm not sure what to think," she admitted.

"Think of yourself for once," Medric said. "And think how you'll thrive in an organization that values your mind more than your political savvy."

Folan smiled.

"And all you'll have to do," Medric continued, "is destroy the *Enterprise*."

Chapter Five

TRYING TO WRENCH HIMSELF FREE of Lotre's tight grip, the Starfleeter first hit the Klingon on his ears, then his neck.

Lotre shoved him away and the smaller man stumbled. A crewman without rank, he noticed. "Tell me," Lotre said, leveling his disruptor at the man's head, "how do I get off this blasted deck?"

The Starfleeter shook his head and scrambled quickly to his feet. He skittered up the corridor and once again Lotre was alone.

Where is *everyone?* And how could he have lost his way? He'd studied the specifications on *Enterprise*. It was possible some intelligence on the vessel was

44

wrong, but *this* much? And where was T'sart? He had to find him . . .

Looking left, then right, Lotre saw no one else. He'd checked every room and not found even a sign of T'sart. And now neither Gorlat nor any of his other men were answering their communicators.

His knuckles were scraped and bleeding, and pain both external and internal bit at him. He walked almost absently, and then, around a bend in the curving walkway, he finally saw the lift that had brought him to this deck.

He rushed to it, the doors barely having time to part fully to allow his width. "Bridge," he ordered it, and as it sped toward deck one, he leaned against the rear wall for the short moment he knew he had.

And the moment dragged on too long. There were only six decks to cross . . . why was he not there yet? "Hold," he ordered, and checked the control panel. Still deck seven. He'd moved, but the computer said he hadn't. What kind of maze was this ship? What in all the hells was going on?

Anger plucked at the veins in his neck and he aimed his weapon at the control panel and fired. So what if the whole damn thing exploded into his face? He didn't care anymore.

In a shower of sparks and debris, the access controls erupted into flame. But he was unharmed. Reflex should not have saved him. Nothing should have saved him—a blast that close at full power should have given him third-degree burns at the very least.

Something was very wrong and instinct told him it

was not his own mind that was warped, but the world around him that had changed.

The air sizzled with heat and smoke. Soot was filling the air, and he choked on it. But would it have killed him? Could he have asphyxiated on it?

He took in a sharp breath, not only steadying himself, but testing a theory . . . to no avail. He needed more determinate evidence.

Playing a very deadly hunch, Lotre kept his disruptor on the vaporize setting and pointed the barrel at his own head. He fingered the trigger and the whine of the weapon bounced off the lift walls and filled his ears.

A flash of light—and he was not at all dead.

His lungs pounding out fury with each breath, Lotre growled his understanding. "Of course." He shook his head in tortured regret.

"Shut up and lie down!" Dr. Beverly Crusher didn't have time for bedside manner and Governor Kalor apparently was going to force her to muscle him down onto the biobed near T'sart's.

"Picard, I may have to help save this vile monster's life, but need I stand for such abuse from your doctor?" the Klingon pleaded.

"I don't want you to stand at all," Crusher mumbled. "I told you to lie down."

Kalor huffed and puffed, but Crusher was not made of straw and easily blown down. He did as she said.

She quickly connected him to some contraption that was pulling blood from his very veins, doing something to it, and then injecting it into T'sart's arm.

"Are not there curses like this?"

Picard wondered the same himself. "Is this going to work?" he asked Crusher as she finished configuring a panel on the makeshift apparatus.

"The official medical nomenclature is 'grasping at straws.' " She picked up a medical tricorder and hovered the scanner over Kalor's body. "This is going to weaken you," she told him.

"Picard mentioned that," Kalor said.

"We're also going to raise your temperature," Crusher told him.

Kalor blinked a few times and seemed to be weakening a bit already. "Why?"

Crusher frowned, as she always did when having to talk about artificial diseases designed to be efficient killers. "T'sart's virus reacts to a rise in body temperature. It thrives on it. A devious bit of engineering that causes the body temperature to rise, then prospers on the heat, feeding itself."

"And . . . why must I . . . have a fever." Kalor was slowing down, and T'sart seemed to be stirring. Picard thought that more coincidence than a result of the new treatment. In any case, it was a good sign.

The doctor glanced up at T'sart's bio-monitor and administered a hypospray into Kalor's neck. "Klingon blood runs hotter than a Romulan's," she explained slowly, compensating for Kalor's probably impeded perceptions. "We're giving you a *mild* fever that will be hotter than T'sart's *high* fever."

The Klingon's eyelids were beginning to close. He was being forced to fight a disease not his own—

though inflicted by him on another—and his body was adjusting to the fight. "I still . . . don't see . . . what that will do."

"You're connected to one another. And this . . ." Crusher pointed to the appliance that quietly was manipulating both Kalor's and T'sart's blood. ". . . will keep any foreign elements, other than his virus and your antibodies, from passing between your two bodies." Only when he finally, wearily looked up at the contraption did Crusher stop pointing at it.

"Y-you will not be able to . . ." Kalor seemed as if he was searching for the right word. "Fuh-filter . . . out the virus cuh-completely . . . from his organs."

The doctor seemed to both shrug and shake her head. "We're not that sure. The virus may move to your body when it senses the higher temperature."

"Thuh-that could take s-some time." Kalor sounded cold, tired, and Picard thought he might begin shivering any moment.

"It might take some time, yes," Crusher said softly, and her warmer bedside manner was showing. Care for everyone, compassion for those who deserved it? Picard wondered. After all, Kalor was the one who infected T'sart in the first place.

"Just rest," she told Kalor, then looked up at Picard. "The cure could kill him," she said, "and it might not even save T'sart."

Picard began to answer but his combadge chirped and he turned his attention to that.

"Spock to Picard."

"Picard here."

"Captain, we have a concern."

"With?"

"Our rendezvous with Commander Riker."

"I'll be right there." He tapped his combadge again and looked to Crusher.

She was standing at the foot of Kalor's biobed. "I'm coming with you," she told him, in that tone that suggested he shouldn't take the time to argue.

"Can you get away?" Picard indicated her two very important patients.

"Would I leave if I couldn't?" she snapped—or came close to it anyway.

Picard pursed his lips. She wouldn't. "Come along."

Crusher close behind him, Picard went directly to Spock at the science station from the turbolift. "Spock?"

"We are close to the rendezvous coordinates." The Vulcan stood to greet Picard with presumably troublesome news. It wasn't Spock's expression that broadcast that, but the fact that whatever information he did have, he didn't want to share over the comm.

"Why only close?" Picard asked.

"There is a dead zone—"

Picard cut him off with the pertinent question. "And Riker's runabout?"

"We don't know. There is a vessel near the center of the event. The mass would be right for the runabout."

The captain now noticed that the bridge personnel were gathered around, and Geordi La Forge.

"Life signs?" Picard asked, and his throat felt very dry.

"Indeterminate. Our sensors will not penetrate the

zone enough to know. But we read only null power levels on the vessel." Spock's words were chosen carefully, Picard thought—for accuracy, not for impact.

The idea of the runabout trapped in a dead zone staggered the captain. Riker, Troi, even Data would be affected. "How long might they have been there?"

"There is no way to know," Spock said with the slightest shake of his head. "Our sensors are greatly impeded by the dead zone itself."

Chest feeling tight, Picard turned toward the forward viewscreen. He looked past Rossi and Shapiro at conn and ops, who were angled around to look at him, and instead watched the static view of the starscape before them. "How close can we get to them without falling into the dead zone ourselves?"

"Two million kilometers." Spock didn't check the calculation. "We're that close now. We attempted to get the most accurate sensor readings possible."

Geordi La Forge stepped forward. "Captain, I'm sure we could get to it with another shuttle. I can rig an extra thruster pack and bring the whole thing out."

"How long would that take?" Picard asked.

Hesitating just a moment, Geordi said, "Ten, maybe twelve hours?"

The captain shook his head. "We can't spare the time." And as he said it, the words hurt and even shocked him as much as it seemed they did the rest of his crew. It was against his instinct, it was against his will, and his heart.

But without knowing how much time the galaxy had . . . what other choice did he have?

"Jean-Luc, surely you're not suggesting we just

leave them." Beverly Crusher didn't sound angry so much as indignantly outraged, and he knew her well enough to tell the subtle difference.

"We can't spare the time," Picard repeated more emphatically.

"Then leave me behind," Geordi offered. "With a shuttle and the right supplies—"

"You could find yourself stranded as well," Spock said.

Picard nodded his agreement. "We can't know the age of this dead zone. You could put inside and not be able to get back, even with chemical thrusters."

"It's worth the risk." Geordi stepped toward his captain and let the man see his determined visage.

"No," Picard said a bit more quietly than he would have liked, "it's not. Not to this mission. I need you— *all* of you—to see this through."

"What about Commander Riker and Counselor Troi, captain?" Geordi asked. "What about Data?"

Picard understood. These people were not merely friends and crewmates, but as long as they'd served together, they were family. "Spock, without life-support, how long before . . . they would freeze?"

"Three hours."

The captain nodded slowly, sadly. "Your attempt, Mr. La Forge. How long would it take?"

Geordi didn't answer, but deflected Picard's question into a new request. "What about Data, sir? He doesn't need life-support. He'll be alive."

"Alive," Crusher mumbled mostly to herself, "and watching the others die."

The guilt of having to send people to their deaths

was one every captain dealt with at some point. Picard was no stranger to it. But this obvious torture that Data might go through . . . "God help him, I hope he turns off his emotion chip."

Geordi sighed, loudly, plaintively. "Knowing Data, sir . . . he won't."

That, Picard thought, was perhaps correct. Data wouldn't want to disrespect his own loss by not feeling it.

A small alert signal wrenched Picard's attention away from that thought, and he was grateful for it.

"What is it?"

Spock was already bent over his console. "Two vessels," he said, looking up for only an instant. "Decloaking."

"Shields!" Picard quickly jumped down to the lower deck and his command chair.

"Design is Klingon, sir," Chamberlain reported.

The captain swiveled toward him. "Kalor's ship?"

Chamberlain nodded. "One of them."

"Alert them to the presence of the dead zone. Transmit the known coordinates." Picard then turned to Spock. "How did you detect them with their cloaks?" he asked.

Spock jabbed a view commands into his console and turned toward the captain. "I did not. I've reconfigured the main deflector array to send out a subspace frequency wave to help detect dead zones before we encounter them. When we scan ahead and fail to receive back resonance from that frequency, we know a dead zone, or in this case, a cloaked vessel, is in range of our main deflector array."

Picard nodded. "Radio detecting and ranging. RADAR, but with subspace radio."

"A somewhat inaccurate, but serviceable analogy," Spock said.

"Parl is hailing us, sir," said Chamberlain from tactical.

"On screen."

"Captain Picard—"

"I thought Kalor ordered you to secure your sector and report your situation to the next governorship."

"He did. And he also had us reconnoiter for you. The next ten sectors are clear. After that, reports are that the Romulan fleet has pulled back."

"Pulled back?" Picard felt his brow furrow and he leaned forward in his seat. "Explain."

"Word is there are a large number of tightly placed dead zones around the Romulan homeworld and the most populated systems. The Romulan Senate fears this is prelude to invasion."

"From the Federation?" Picard asked.

"From everyone," Parl said quite soberly. *"They are protecting themselves. In any case, your way is clear."*

"You're sure of this?" the captain asked.

"I've seen it myself. We offer assistance. We would accompany you."

Picard nodded, and his heart felt no better than before. "Follow from behind. We have a way to see the dead zones. And run cloaked—a convoy would draw more attention."

Parl nodded. *"How is the governor?"* he asked.

"He's assisting us . . . in another manner." Picard

wasn't sure what Kalor had told Parl, and what he'd want Parl to know, so he remained vague.

"We are, at his order, under your command, Picard."

The captain nodded. He'd need the help. "Stand by to get under way. Picard out."

It was all for nothing, Picard thought as he stared passed the Klingon vessel and into the unremarkable dead zone. If the Romulan fleet had pulled back, *Enterprise* didn't even need the element he'd sent Riker and Troi and Data to retrieve.

He'd sent his crew on a suicide mission, and there wasn't now even a reason for them to have made the attempt.

If he lived, how would he live with that?

"Set the course," Picard ordered, mustering the most authoritative tone he could. "The Caltiskan system."

"Course set," Rossi said.

The captain slumped back in the center seat and made the smallest of gestures with his right hand. "Engage. Maximum warp."

Chapter Six

Private vessel *Loa-var*
Romulan space
Sector 36

"MR. DATA? ARE YOU ALL RIGHT?" Whispering, Tobin opened the access panel just outside his vessel's bridge and peered within. The Starfleet lieutenant commander had been hiding from the repair crew by concealing himself behind a false bulkhead.

"I am well, thank you," came Data's almost cheerful response.

Tobin shook his head and stood back to allow Data to escape from the access alcove. "It's hard to believe you didn't suffocate."

"I do not breathe," he said matter-of-factly. "I am an android." Data did not attempt to remove himself, but instead stood his ground, his pale yellow face cast half in shadow.

"It's not easy to remember that you're not a bioform," Tobin admitted sheepishly.

"It is easy for me," Data told him.

"Of course," Tobin replied. "Aren't you going to come out now?"

"I would rather stay until all repair personnel are off the vessel."

Tobin looked around suspiciously and he felt his heart quicken. "I thought they were. Aren't they finished yet? I got word that repairs were complete."

Standing oddly at attention behind the opening in the wall, Data's response seemed straightforward and yet surreal. "The barantium cargo was loaded, but in monitoring communication frequencies of the repair crew, I gleaned that repairs were finished, and then later seemingly not."

A slight panic rose in Tobin's chest and he looked away. "As if they finished, then decided they'd done so too early?"

Data cocked his head to one side and when Tobin looked back he saw more of the android's pale yellow skin which seemed to almost glow in the low light of the powered-down ship. "That is one possibility."

Hesitating a moment, Tobin tried to concentrate. What did all this mean? How would they all escape if the authorities were onto them? "Can you fix what they'd apparently repaired and then un-repaired?" he asked.

"Of course," Data said. "I broke it in the first place."

Sadly true, Tobin thought to himself. "How fast can you work?"

"My speed and manual dexterity are, on average, seven point three times better than an average human's; five point seven times better than an average Vulcan's or Romulan's; six point—"

"I see the pattern, thank you." Tobin stood back again and this time Data took the invitation to exit his protective alcove. "They're not going to let us leave spacedock in disrepair, even if we wanted to. It's a regulation. They'd fire on is if we did. And if we fix it, they'll want to know how. But I think you need to fix it anyway. So that we're ready for any contingency."

Walking past Tobin, Data seemed to be making his way toward the aft section and the transporter alcove. "We should beam Commander Riker and Counselor Troi back to the ship."

The Romulan shook his head. "Not while in spacedock. The energy surge would be noticed and investigated, and perhaps even stopped in transit when the station puts their shields up. Someone caught in a beam would die."

Data stopped and turned to Tobin. "We must get them back to the ship. If we break out of spacedock once repaired, we will not be able to beam them back while cloaked, or with our shields up."

"I know. I'm not sure what to do," Tobin admitted.

"I will repair the ship," Data told him. "You must go to Commander Riker and advise him of the situation."

Tobin sighed. "They might not beam me down. I'll need a shuttle or some vessel to get to the surface."

"Please find one. I will expedite repairs." The android turned and walked toward the small engineering access room.

Find one, he tells me, Tobin thought. *In the Federation, are spaceships of such abundance it is as if they hatch from eggs?*

The Romulan shook his head despondently. *Find one,* his mind echoed, and he sighed.

As made his way past one of the security stations, Tobin was nodded to by the guard, and he felt obligated to nod back.

The situation, he decided, was bad. He knew the look the guard had—the stance of a cautious sentry who was eyeing a suspect. Security personnel had two manners about them: they either ignored you, or watched you with interest. Tobin was not being ignored.

He was now sure that something had gone wrong. He had an idea what, but couldn't be sure and anyway it didn't much matter now.

Find a ship, he thought. But what ship could he just "find"?

He needed to be calm—he was letting his mind rush too fast. Just because people were watching him didn't mean they'd see more than was obvious. If he could just keep himself from being conspicuous . . .

A difficult task considering where he was headed: one of the restricted airlocks for docked repair and maintenance vehicles. If stopped and questioned as to why he was there, certainly he could say he was lost. But he'd be detained for some time, and eventually they'd figure out all they needed to.

Very risky. He wondered if it had been a mistake to backtrack to meet the Federation shuttle. How foolish had he been to do that?

If the Starfleeters were correct about what was happening . . . well, it was a good cause, was it not?

But how was he supposed to find a ship he could use to retrieve Riker? And what about Deanna?

Tobin had never been in the military. It took him years of planning to arrange his escape from Romulan space—and obviously that plan was lacking. Certainly he wasn't used to thinking quickly on his feet.

Now he had to: someone was walking toward him.

"What are you doing here?" the man demanded. He wore the garb of a maintenance worker. He was not security, and probably not skilled in self-defense.

Without more thought than that, Tobin attacked the larger man. He leapt forward and grabbed him around the neck, pulling him to the deck.

"What are you doing?" the tech yelped as he fell to the ground with a grunt.

Tobin made the tightest fist he could and pounded the man in the head, attempting to knock him unconscious. All he managed to do was hurt his knuckles—badly.

Growling in anger, the maintenance worker tossed Tobin against the bulkhead and pain exploded along the smaller Romulan's spine.

That was foolish, he thought as the other man now lunged at him.

In fear, Tobin crammed his eyes shut and shrank away from his attacker. Frightened, he curled his body into a compact ball.

Thwap. He heard a thump, a grunt, and then felt the man collapse on him.

Motionless, Tobin didn't even breathe. He felt the maintenance man's breath, however—shallow and slower with every thin huff.

He waited a moment . . . and when the man didn't stir, he pushed out from under him and rolled away.

Tobin opened his eyes wide in amazement. The man had lunged at him, hit the bulkhead, and knocked himself out.

He pushed the man over and began searching the fallen man's pockets. *He must have a code key. He* must!

He did—in one of his tunic pockets. Tobin read it, found it was for the airlock at the end of the hall, and scrambled into a sloppy run.

Luck . . . it was all he had. He didn't know how to fight—the one he'd stupidly chosen to battle had luckily knocked himself out in his anger. Luck seemed to be all he really had going for him, and it was dumb luck at that.

But he'd take it—and he'd take the man's ship— whatever it was.

Fumbling with the cardkey, he ungracefully put it against the scanner and the airlock slowly clicked and whirred open. He squeezed himself between the door and the bulkhead before it was fully open and exploded onto the ship.

Also stupid, he thought. Certainly there was no one else aboard, but how did he know that until he barged right into the cabin? He didn't, but once again dumb luck was working in his favor.

He closed the hatch again, this time from the inside,

and then spun around in the small cockpit. Trash was strewn about and the overwhelming odor was the oily, industrial smell of the man he'd stolen it from. Kicking discarded food containers out of his way, Tobin sat down in the pilot's seat.

Finally, here was where luck gave way to experience: he knew the controls of the ship. They were hardly different from other industrial vessels, and in fact not too dissimilar to those of his own ship. If anything, they were less complex.

There was no need to get clearance from space-dock—maintenance vessels came and went as they pleased. Tobin merely sent the right protocols to the docking computer and was released.

It was while looking at an internal diagnostic panel as he made his way toward the planet that he first realized just what kind of vessel he'd just stolen: a tractor-tug.

His heart sank in despair. A tractor-tug. Those didn't normally go planetside. Not only might it be noticed . . . but he might not even be able to get it through the atmosphere.

He set the course nevertheless. What choice did he have?

As he began a descent toward the planet, his shields flaring with fire from the friction against the photosphere, he saw the alerts from the spacedock, and the orders on the comm for him to return.

He ignored them. What was he doing? They would find him. They would *kill* him. Not only had he planned to escape—he'd aided and abetted the Federation.

Tobin felt a fool.

A klaxon blared in his ears. Shields were failing. The burning ship would mask spacedock from getting a sensor or weapon lock on the tug . . . but it was a futile effort. The ship would burn up before he was able to land it.

The vessel's coolant systems couldn't compensate as the hull began to superheat. Sweat began to bubble on Tobin's forehead, and as system after system failed under a boil of friction, he knew the only way he'd land would be as a lump of charcoal in a fractured hull.

His escape plan had failed.

Think! What can I do? Don't panic! he chastised himself.

He had some systems left. Shields were gone, but was there an escape pod? No, not in such a small ship.

Hull temperature was well past tolerances. He was sweating bathtubs and could barely see. Structural integrity was weakening. Life support was failing. The only thing available was the useless tractor emitters. He didn't need to tow a ship, he needed to—

Wait. Wait! He could use this—use the tractor emitters, couldn't he? They could push as well as pull.

Tobin's hands galloped over the control panel. If he could do it—if he had time before the tug came apart . . .

Beneath him the tractor beam spread itself out, carving a bowl of vacuum by pushing away the atmosphere molecules. The air on the underside of the beam perimeter was burning away, but the heat and friction was kept away from the hull.

It was working: functions were coming back online as coolant systems began coping again.

Still, he was tight with tension until he could slow

the ship adequately and was far enough into the atmosphere to level his descent. When he was flying normal and evenly, Tobin huffed out a sigh and collapsed back into his seat.

And a moment later, he sat rigid again with anxiety. Perhaps the spacedock security had not tracked onto the planet, but soon they would begin again with ease. He needed to find Riker—and quickly.

Riker had battled the Borg—and won. He'd traveled time, and come back to tell the story. He'd been close to death, and lived. And while he'd been anxious, afraid, and sometimes even terrified, he'd never really let it show.

But Nien saw all.

"Don't be nervous," she told him. "I don't care that you're human. I just want the truth. That is all."

He sighed. She was far too much like his aunt. Here he was, on an exceedingly important covert mission, and he felt as if he were letting down a family member.

How could he tell her?

What *should* he tell her?

By asking a question, he could delay having to tell her anything. "How did you know?"

She smiled, perhaps pleased with the confirmation of her deduction. "I recognized your language," she told him in heavily accented English. "My husband was in the diplomatic corps for many years. There was a time when the government allowed me to travel with him."

"Is that why you're not afraid of me?" He didn't

quite look at her. He looked past her, then down at his half full dinner plate.

Nien waited until his eyes met hers. "One doesn't live two hundred and seventeen years without learning something about people."

"So, I'm human." Riker shrugged and thought perhaps he might try the nonchalant tack. "Why do you think I'm something more than I say?"

She dabbed at the corners of her lips with her napkin, again unnecessarily, but Riker imagined it was some habit she had when a napkin was at hand. "You don't exactly carry yourself like a vagrant. You're cultured. When I showed you the library you seemed surprised I had non-Romulan volumes of literature. To know that meant you recognized the authors' names and titles of the works."

Okay, so Riker needed to work on his covert mission personality skills. He'd failed to role-play. "Is that all?"

Nien shook her head, a small motion, delicate. "You were looking more at the security console itself than the monitors when I was showing you the sensor screens of the entire estate."

He bowed his head in acceptance. "My mistake."

She dismissed the notion of his error with the wave of her hand. "Old women with little to do become very observant."

"I have the feeling you were just as perceptive when you were young."

Blushing just a touch, Nien lowered her gaze and smiled. "In any case . . ."

"What now?" Riker asked, pushing his plate away. He certainly didn't want any more dinner. If anything he'd expected to be beamed out by now. What was taking so long? They couldn't miss the rendezvous with *Enterprise*.

"If you're asking if I intend to turn you in, the answer is no." She reached out her hand across the table. Not taking his hand, just showing her own as a symbol of friendship and closeness. "But I would like to know why you're here. I assume you're not staying."

He sighed heavily. She was too smart for him. "No, I can't stay."

"Can you tell me why you're here? Why you did this?"

Dourly, Riker shook his head. "I can't."

"Can you—"

Rrrrrrrrrrr . . . A rumble from outside the house shook the table and the wall hangings and even the pots in the kitchen.

"Oh, my! What's happening!"

It wasn't an earthquake. Riker knew that sound—or sounds like it. It was a ship, a big one—probably right on top of the house.

He shoved himself away from the table. "Do you have any weapons?"

Rising, Nien followed him toward the window. "We're not allowed."

"Figures," Riker grumbled, and peeked out through the window blinds. "It's a vessel. I don't recognize the design. Do you?" He opened the blinds with thumb and forefinger and moved to one side so she could look out.

Nien squinted out into the yard. "No. It's awfully large. It's not a shuttle."

A weapon. He needed a weapon. He glanced toward the kitchen. A knife? It was better than nothing. "It doesn't even look like it's a vessel that's supposed to land."

"No," Tobin said. "It's not." As if he beamed in—but he hadn't seemed to—the Romulan man stood a few feet before them.

Clapping her hands over her mouth, Nien gasped. Riker just stared with incredulity.

Upswept brows arching into his bangs, Tobin shrugged. "The front door was open."

"What the hell are you doing here?" Riker demanded, crooking a thumb over his shoulder, toward the window. "And in that?"

Tobin blew out a puff of breath. "Long story."

Taking his arm and walking toward the main door with him—and Nien following—Riker felt a sudden gush of relief. Maybe this wasn't a beam-up, but if they hurried they could still make the rendezvous in time. "Give me the short version."

"Spacedock security is suspicious. Their repair crews had the ship fixed, then claimed they did not. Watched as we were, we couldn't scan for human life signs, let alone beam you up."

They moved into the yard, the setting sun casting long shadows as they walked. "Data?"

"Repairing the vessel," Tobin said, huffing a bit as he tried to keep up with Riker's brisk stride. Nien was probably falling behind.

"And Deanna?"

Tobin hesitated a moment and so Riker stopped and turned.

"What? Tell me what."

"I don't know where she is," Tobin said. "I had this address for your buyer, but hers had three different estates. I could not check them all."

Making his way toward the vessel again, Riker couldn't help but be torn between his concern for Deanna, and his concern for the mission. "This ship doesn't have sensors?"

"Not of the quality we would need to find her specific life sign."

"Then we'll have to check all three places," Riker decided. "I'm not leaving her behind."

"We don't have the time!" Tobin pleaded. "Surely they've tracked me here—"

"That's not where our time problem is. We have to meet—" Riker stopped himself before he could name the *Enterprise* specifically in front of Nien, who amazingly had managed to keep up pretty well. "—my ship," he finished awkwardly.

"We'll be lucky to just stay alive," Tobin said. "We have to lay low for at least a few hours, or a day. And maybe get word to Deanna to do the same."

"No, we're leaving now. Come on." Riker stopped just before vessel's main hatch and turned back toward Nien. "I'm sorry," he told her.

She smiled. "So am I."

He took her shoulders and gave them an affectionate

squeeze. "I guess you knew I wouldn't be here for ten years."

Nodding, she said, "I also didn't think you'd be leaving today, in this manner."

"This is . . ." He wanted to tell her, but now there was not time. "It's very important—what we're doing."

Nien nodded acceptance. "I gather that." She paused a moment, then added, "Can I help?"

He shook his head and let his hands drop to his sides. "I don't see how."

The woman looked down, thinking a moment; then her bright eyes bounced back up. "Who bought your friend?"

Riker turned to Tobin. "Name?"

"Tar Galal."

Nien nodded. "Ah, I *do* know him."

"Know him well? Well enough to be invited into his home?" Riker asked.

She shrugged. "My grandson was a contemporary of his. I never liked him, even as a boy. Smarmy, ill-mannered."

"That's the guy," Riker said. "Do you know where he'd be now?"

"This time of the year? He would be in his western estate."

"Have you ever been there?"

"On a few occasions."

He stroked his chin thoughtfully and considered the possibilities. "Can I make you a hostage?" he asked her.

"So I won't get in trouble? I won't, trust me. I will help you of my own will."

Riker gestured toward the hatch in an "after you" motion.

"You're an extraordinary woman, Nien."

With only a little help from Riker, she lifted herself gracefully aboard the ship. "My dear child, you should have seen me a hundred and fifty years ago."

Chapter Seven

"This ship is very conspicuous. It will be noticed."
Tobin was complaining, and his tone was beginning to
get on Riker's nerves.

"We're not going to buzz his house," Riker said,
studying the Romulan controls and watching Tobin's
hands as he piloted. "We'll need to put down in a covered area."

"He has a garden. It's very lush. There should be
enough cover there." Without a chair to accommodate
her, Nien was sitting on the long lip of one of the control consoles.

Oddly, Riker felt a pang of guilt that he couldn't give
her his own seat. "And you thought I was just taking
you along for your looks."

"Flatterer." She patted him lightly on the shoulder.

"No, I'm telling you, Deanna will be jealous. She'll

take one look at you and wonder how I got some beauty queen to buy me."

She nearly giggled. "Enough of your blandishment, young man!"

"Yes, ma'am," he said, and grinned deeply.

"This is foolhardy." Tobin's worry slashed across the nice moment. "We will be caught."

"Maybe. We can't afford to worry about it. We just continue the mission for as long as we're able." As the countryside rolled underneath, Riker couldn't take much time to appreciate the scenery. He was keeping his eye out for security crafts he wasn't worried about.

"I'm going to worry, if you don't mind," Tobin said quietly, more to himself than Riker.

"Over here," Nien said, rising and pointing at the main viewscreen. "See the grotto?"

Riker saw it: a semicircle of trees on one side, with what looked like a stylized gazebo on the other. There would barely be enough room to land the tug, but the trees would obscure anyone in the house from seeing. That wouldn't help them with any sensor cameras, but Riker had noticed Nien's sensors were very basic, and mostly for video. He was wagering that this estate would have the same setup. At least the area was far enough away that the noise would probably not be heard all the way to the main house.

"That should do," Riker said finally.

"Is it tall enough?" Tobin asked. "The top of the ship will show." Riker noticed the Romulan was biting his lower lip. He couldn't really blame Tobin for being on edge. Most people didn't involve themselves in life-and-death situations on a regular basis.

"It'll be fine. It's far enough away they won't hear us land. Just set us down. We'll worry about the rest later."

"I don't see that you ever worry," Tobin said, but not so much with irritation as it was with regard.

"Like I said, we can't afford to." That was mostly bravado. He *was* worried . . . just about the rendezvous more than any number of third-rate, backwater Romulan rent-a-guards.

Holding his breath as Tobin landed the ship, Riker hoped he was right and the loud hum of the engines would be muffled by the trees.

Once the ship had touched down with a soft thunk, Riker turned to Nien. "I can't ask you to go farther."

"You can't stop me," she told him. "Who will be more conspicuous approaching the main door? A human, or a Romulan woman and her two servants?"

Riker shook his head. She was brave, but this wasn't her fight. "We don't have any weapons. I can't protect you."

"Oh! That's right!" Tobin said excitedly and pulled a phaser and Riker's combadge out from a small storage compartment near the helm.

Riker accepted the weapon and communicator with a grin. "Tobin, sometimes I've very glad we happened upon you."

"Someone should be," Tobin mumbled.

Nien snapped her fingers and got his attention. "Young man?"

"Yes, m'lady?" Tobin replied.

"Stop being snotty."

Riker laughed, and Tobin couldn't help but smile as well. It obviously sounded as funny in their language as it had in Riker's.

He flicked the switch that opened the hatch. Riker went first, followed by Tobin.

"You okay?" Riker asked him.

"She was right," he said quietly. "I was acting improperly. Your mission is just. I must help."

"She doesn't even know what my mission is."

Only a little surprised, Tobin watched Nien as she lowered her head unnecessarily and passed through the hatchway. "No? I suppose she doesn't need to. It would seem she knows *you*."

After that, the three were silent as they made their way toward the main doorway at the front of the house.

Once on the uppermost level of the porch, they heard an automatic chime summon someone to the door.

Soon after, a non-automatic door opened with a click.

"Greetings." A Romulan, wearing a slightly more fancy set of servants garb.

"Jolan true," Nien said, only bowing her head a little. Probably showing respect to the estate, but not the servant. "I am here to see the master of the house."

The servant—perhaps he was a butler—shook his head slowly. "The master has left word he is not to be disturbed."

She nodded acceptance of that and looked like she might turn away, then looked back up. "Might I stay and wait for his audience?" she asked politely.

"I'm sorry, m'lady. That would not be well advised."

He spoke in a monotone. Riker could glean no emotion from his words.

"I see."

"If you'd like to leave words of your visit, I shall relay it."

Riker touched Nien on her shoulder and she stepped out of the way. "Hey, don't disappoint my aunt."

"Who—"

The guard fell, and all it took was a whap on his chin. With a lot of shoulder behind it. Riker shoved the fallen man out of his way and let Nien and Tobin pass.

"I thought for certain you'd just stun him," Tobin said, still looking quite surprised at Riker's fast action.

"Phasers make noise." He didn't see any place to really hide the butler, so he propped him in the corner by the door and whispered "Rest well" as he turned to look up the foyer.

"You're just leaving him there?" Tobin asked.

Riker shrugged. "He asked us to leave word of our visit."

"You're quite strong." Nien was whispering and Riker realized she was also walking very lightly, not quite on tiptoe.

"It's more knowing how to use your muscle than how much actual muscle you have." At a crossway where a hall went two ways, Riker looked to Nien to lend him some direction. She gestured toward one and they all followed the recommendation.

"I noticed the guard, butler—whichever—didn't have a weapon." Riker was looking and listening for others, but he heard and saw nothing.

"I told you, it's not allowed," Nien reminded.

"That gives us the advantage."

Tobin was walking in their direction but kept turning around to watch for anyone coming up behind them. "I'm beginning to think you don't need one."

"We're not out of here yet," Riker said. "Not by a long shot." He had that feeling he'd gotten in the Academy, when he had a long tedious paper to write, and was only on the first page. It wouldn't be a difficult paper, but it needed to be written and there was much to do before he was finished. Finding Deanna was the first page. They had to get back to the spacedock and get the ship, and then get back to the *Enterprise* in time . . . miles to go before they slept.

"There's a suspicious lack of people around here," Riker noticed.

"Apparently he wanted to be alone with—" Tobin stopped himself in midsentence. "I—I'm sorry, it was a poor choice of words."

"I know what he wanted," Riker said, his lips curled down into a frown.

"Private quarters would be far from the front entrance," Nien said. She knew what Tar Galal wanted too.

At the end of the hall was a closed door. The only closed door they'd seen so far.

Riker approached and quietly tried the old-fashioned knob.

"It's locked?" Tobin asked.

"Not for long." He pulled out his weapon and lightly pushed Nien back. "I'm going to have to phaser this."

"That will bring everyone in the house down on us."

Tobin was sounding very nervous again. Not snotty this time, just tense.

"I know." Riker motioned toward one of the rooms where the doors were open. "Use one of those windows. Get back to that ship. Bring it around for a quick escape. When this phaser goes off, noise won't matter."

"Give me five minutes."

Riker shook his head. "You've got until you're out the window. I'm not leaving her a moment longer."

Tobin nodded and skittered into the nearest room.

Listening for the opening of the window, Riker hesitated, watched for anyone coming, then admonished Nien to stand back even farther.

He took a few steps back as well and phasered the door lock with a very thin beam.

The lock broke with a loud *pop* and the door swung open. He moved into the room, phaser up, looking for the fat Romulan's face, and—

"Will!" Deanna was in the center of the large bed, reading a book.

"Deanna?" Riker's face felt warm and his skin was tight.

"I'm glad to see you. I was getting worried." She closed her book, dropped her legs over the side of the bed, and stood.

He looked at the book on the bed, then back to her. "I can see that."

She waved her hand at the book, dismissing it. "I mean I expected to be beamed up by now."

Riker shook his head. "Change in plans. Where's your 'employer'?"

"Oh, him," Deanna said disdainfully. "He tried to get fresh with me."

" 'Fresh'?" Riker's muscles snapped taut. "Where is he?" he almost growled.

"Locked in the closet."

Obviously hearing their voices, he began knocking on the walls, ordering them to let him out.

Deanna sighed. "Oh, don't start the shouting again. We talked about that, remember? It gives me a headache."

"She reminds me of me," Nien told Riker, smirking.

He looked from the closet, to Deanna, and back to the closet. "I should have known," he said and walked toward the closet. "In here?"

"Yes. What are you going to do?"

"I want to see him," Riker said.

Deanna sighed. "Will—"

"In here?"

"Yes, but—"

Riker opened the door. The same fat Romulan from earlier in the day was sitting on the floor in the back of the closet. When he saw the door open he immediately jumped up. He moved well for someone his size. "It's about time—" he began, then noticed Riker's face. "Who are you?" he demanded.

"Her boyfriend," Riker said angrily and slammed the Romulan in the nose with his closed fist.

The Romulan stumbled back and then finally fell.

"That was very . . . male of you."

"You bring out the savage in me, *Imzadi*," Riker said with a grin.

She rolled her eyes. "Flatterer."

Sharing a glance with Nien, Riker said, "So I'm told."

"There are others coming," Nien said from the doorway to the hall.

"Who's she?" Deanna asked of Nien.

"My 'employer.' "

"Hello, my dear," Nien said politely.

Deanna smiled in return. "Hello." Riker could tell that Deanna also liked Nien instantly.

"Close that door," Riker told her. "We'll use the window."

"What window?" Deanna gestured around the room, showing there was none.

"Wonderful. What kind of room doesn't have windows?"

Deanna crossed her arms against her chest. "Interior rooms."

They heard footsteps padding up hallway outside.

"I could phaser them, but if one of them *does* have a weapon, and it's not set to stun, I don't want to risk either of you." Riker frowned and looked up and then around the room, searching for another door, a vent, an attic access—anything.

"Perhaps I could talk to them," Nien offered.

At the door, at least two Romulan voices could be heard. "Lord? Are you all right?"

"I've met them," Deanna said. "They're not exactly listening types."

Riker dragged the Romulan off the floor and let him sit on the edge of the bed, next to Nien. He put his phaser close to the Romulan man's head. "Call off your guards."

"My servants."

"Whatever." Riker nudged him with the phaser. "Do it."

Tar Galal didn't look very scared. That wasn't good. "Why should I do as you want?" he asked. "So you can use me as a hostage to escape and then kill me when my usefulness ends?"

"I haven't killed her yet." Riker indicated Nien with a jerk of his head, leaving his phaser trained unerringly on the Romulan.

"Perhaps because she's a woman. I will not help you."

And by his tone, Riker knew he wouldn't.

"Be smart, child. Can't you see this is a matter of import?" When Nien spoke to the other Romulan it wasn't with the same tone she'd used to call Riker "child." That had been kind and warm. This was rather vacant. She wasn't the best liar on the planet.

"Silence, old woman." The Romulan man spat. "I need no help from ancient whores."

His arm acting almost independently, Riker lashed out in anger and backhanded the other man across the jaw.

"How many floors in this house?"

Galal dabbed at a trickle of green blood that came from a corner of his mouth. "Three."

Riker tapped his combadge. "Got that, Tobin?"

"Understood."

"What are you doing?" Galal asked.

"I can't phaser through two floors and not expect to have the roof cave in on me."

"I don't understand." Galal looked truly concerned and confused.

"You will."

It began with one small creaking sound, then rolled into many such noises until it became a low rumble. Riker imagined it was what a tornado must sound like, without the wind. Wood snapped, and metal too, as the top two levels of the house were peeled back and lifted away. The night sky lay above and they could look up at it easily—debris and dust did not fall in on them. It was all held in the tractor field Tobin had cast so precisely that even the light fixture from the bedroom ceiling was whisked away, but the pillows on the bed were completely undisturbed.

There was a crash somewhere outside the house as Tobin dropped the entire top of the estate somewhere off in the distance.

The home's owner stood in awe. "You're insane."

The night wind pouring down into the room, Riker couldn't help but smile just a bit. "You ain't seen nothin' yet." He frisked the man a moment, and when he didn't find what he wanted, he looked around the room.

"What are you doing?" Galal demanded. "What do you want from me?"

By their expressions, Deanna and Nien were wondering the same.

"Stealing the keys to your flitter." Riker spied the keycard on the dresser and grabbed it with his free hand.

"What? What is he doing?" Galal asked Deanna, as if she'd answer him.

"Put him back in the closet, will you?" Riker asked.

Deanna led him back into the enclosure. "My pleasure." She locked him in.

"He brought you here in a vessel," Riker said. "Do you know where it's kept?"

She nodded.

"Lead the way." He motioned to the bed. "A small jump over the wall and we're out."

Deanna took a step toward the bed as Riker turned to Nien and took her hand.

"I've got to leave you here," Riker whispered. "But I'm sure he bought the idea you were a hostage."

"You didn't need to hit him on my account," Nien said, squeezing his hand in hers. "He is an insolent juvenile, in mind if not in age."

"I *did* need to hit him," Riker assured her. "But I'm sorry for all this."

She looked up at him, her eyes alive and understanding. "What you're doing is important, is it not?"

"Very."

"And it will not harm my people." She wasn't really asking a question. It was as if she knew.

"It will help everyone in the galaxy," he said.

"Then you go with my blessing, Riker. And your need for sorrow is not warranted." She patted his hand and smiled sweetly. "My only regret is that I shan't see you again."

"If there's a way—" Riker began.

Nien shook her head. "There is not, that much I know. But I will remember you."

He kissed her on the forehead, and backed away. "Take care."

* * *

"I don't like this plan." Tobin was complaining again.

Riker tapped away at the flitter's controls. "It's not really your ship, Tobin."

"I don't care about the tug. I just don't know that I can accomplish this task."

"You can. You will," Deanna said. It was good to be with her again, Riker thought. He didn't handle Tobin as well by himself.

The tug, bigger, faster, and certainly more powerful, streaked into orbit with the rich Romulan's shuttle far behind. It was much more than a flitter, Riker thought. Most flitters were not spaceworthy. This was more a personal space yacht, with many comforts, but no offensive weapons.

There were no weapons, per se, on the tug either. But as Riker well knew, almost anything could be *used* as a weapon, especially a vessel that had the power to tow other, larger ships.

"Just keep control for long enough, Tobin. They'll swarm the tug quickly, I'm sure," Riker said. His own controls were easy enough and as Tobin slowed the tug in front of them, Riker eased back on the yacht's throttle. He inwardly chuckled at the idea of that—a throttle on an energy-based craft. Despite the antique control it was all computer-controlled, of course. No doubt it was intended to give the owner the "feeling" of hand-controlling all that power. And it did. Too bad the *Enterprise* didn't come with an option set.

"They're hailing the tug," Tobin called.

Riker smiled. "Don't answer. Let them come to you."

And so they did. Within moments four small security shuttles were streaking toward the tug. They fired warning shots that sped past the ship and dissipated into the darkness of space. The shuttles were careful not to fire in line of the planet. Probably not because they feared that such a small disruptor shot would make its way through the atmosphere, but because it could send a satellite off into space or into a quickly decaying orbit.

The security ships swarmed around the tug, firing potshots and trying to herd it toward the spacedock.

"They're continuing to hail," Tobin said. "It is difficult to keep the tug from not going in the direction they're pushing me."

"Then it's time to push back." Riker moved from one console to another, making calculations and scanning the shuttles.

"Tractor beams are ready," Tobin called.

"I'm sending you the proper distances. Be sure to hold them at this perimiter. Any closer and you could destroy them, any farther and this won't work." It was important to Riker that no one be killed. Not simply because of the Starfleet and Federation moral codes that sought to use the least amount of force necessary, but because . . . perhaps more than ever before, the Romulan adversary had a face. Nien's face, really.

How many of the men aboard those security shuttles had a mother, or aunt or sister such as she? It was too easy, as not only an explorer but a military man, to sometimes paint all opponents with the same wide brush. But the armies and governments of great powers were made of individuals, and those individuals touched other individuals . . . and while that didn't make every government's actions valid or right, it needed to be remembered.

"I understand," Tobin said.

"On my mark." Riker redoubled the yacht's shields, such as they were, and plotted the best course around the shock wave.

"And . . . now, Tobin."

At Riker's command, Tobin initiated the plan. The tug he controlled stopped, and the shuttles surrounding it swept in. Lashing out with tractor beams, the tug pulled in three of the shuttles, and pushed the fourth out so that they were all at the distance Riker had ordered.

Weaponless, the tug used the only defense it had. It exploded.

Debris bubbled forward, careening into space and into the shuttles, snapping and sizzling against their shields in a spastic electrical flutter. Then the shock wave followed, and was for the four small craft a disabling blow.

Their propulsion systems crippled, the shuttles reeled away, all at different angles.

Riker was bent over the yacht's small sensor panel. "All four security vessels . . ."

"What?" Deanna prodded.

"They've lost propulsion and communications. All have life-support intact."

"And the tug?"

Riker shook his head. "Completely destroyed."

"We're approaching the spacedock," Deanna said.

Riker swiveled in his seat as he rose. The yacht

pitched, jostled by stray debris, and he had to steady himself against the bulkhead.

"That worked much better than I expected," Tobin said excitedly as he burst from the aft control room. "We actually did it!"

"Well, we're not home free yet," Riker reminded him.

"No, but I didn't think remote control of such a vessel was even possible! Not without it being detected."

Riker pretended to shine his nails on his tunic. "I still know a few tricks."

"Yes, you certainly do." Tobin smiled in sincere response. Perhaps the man panicked quickly, but got over it quickly as well. Riker got the sense that Tobin was most distressed when he wasn't feeling protected. With Riker and Troi around, and a plan in action, the Romulan was much more at ease.

"Now we clear out and let you go to work," Riker told him. "Deanna?"

She rose and patted Tobin on the arm. "Don't be nervous."

Tobin looked out the main port and stared at the spacedock a long moment. "I will not be," he said finally.

Sharing a glance with Deanna, Riker asked Tobin, "You remember what to do?"

The Romulan paused again, then took to the helm chair. "Yes."

As soon as Riker and Deanna were hidden in the aft control room, Tobin flipped the necessary switches to open a local communications channel.

He steadied himself, cleared his throat. "Spacedock

Central, this is the personal craft *Loa-var.* We request permission to dock for repair."

There was a delay and Riker wondered if they were running some kind of voice check. They had, of course, communicated with Tobin before. On a monitor screen, Riker watched Tobin's tense frame shift awkwardly.

Finally, there was a response. *"Stand by,* Loa-var. *We are having difficulties."*

"Yes, I saw that," Tobin said. "What *was* that?"

Though there was again a delay in the answer, it was rather brief this time. *"None of your concern,* Loa-var. *Your repairs will have to wait. Most of our personnel are dealing with our current situation."*

Tobin laid on the charm. "Of course, of course, I well understand. But I really *am* in a hurry. I'd heard your fees had doubled recently. I know I'd be willing to pay that in full."

Riker nodded his approval. Tobin had an elegant way of offering a bribe. Considering the restrictive culture he lived in, that made sense—in most non-free-market economies there was a large back-door or underground black market based on trade and bribery.

When there was no immediate answer, Tobin added, "Not including any standard gratuity, of course, which would have to accommodate you for any . . . *extra trouble.*"

This time, there was no delay in reaction. *"Docking bay three. Dock and await a technician to contact you."*

"Jolan true," Tobin said. "Jolan true." He closed the comm channel and turned toward the aft.

Riker and Deanna came out of hiding. "We're in," Riker said, and offered his hand for Tobin to shake.

"How will you deal with what security *is* left?" Tobin asked, taking Riker's hand and shaking it.

"You'll see." Riker smiled.

And once their ship was docked, Riker, phaser in hand, was first near the hatch as it opened.

There was only one person waiting for them. Not enough to waste a phaser shot on, Riker punched him in the throat.

The Romulan went down, gurgling and grasping his neck.

Riker nodded at Tobin, a slight smile curling his lips. *"That* is how I'll deal with security."

From there it had been as easy as Riker suspected. They'd seen two more officials on the entire station, and one of those was in the main docking control room. Riker stunned them both and joined Data, Deanna, and Tobin on Tobin's vessel.

In minutes, they were clear, the cloak was functioning, and Riker wanted to hurry.

"We are free," Tobin said. "Navigation is clear." He seemed quite pleased to be back in control of his own vessel.

"Cloak?"

"Stable," Data said, checking a readout on one of the consoles.

Riker sat in one of the chairs to one side and wished he could be at helm, or in a command chair, or anywhere that seemed to have a purpose other than waiting. "Now we have to hurry, people. What's your maximum on this ship?"

Tobin turned toward him. "Warp seven in bursts. Warp six for extended." He looked a bit disappointed in his vessel's ability, as if he wished it should be better than it was.

"We need to push it," Riker said. "Mr. Data, set a course for the rendezvous—maximum warp."

They'd been traveling silently for some time when it happened. The main lights had gone off suddenly.

"We've lost all main power," Tobin complained. He sounded panicky again.

"Battery systems are active, but warp and impulse are offline," Data said, and in the dim emergency lights looked more orange than pale yellow.

"A dead zone," Riker said, and dreaded the idea. He felt a thin film of cold sweat begin to develop in the small of his back. "What about thrusters?"

"Not responding." Tobin shook his head quickly and if he kept it up Riker thought it might snap off. "We're dead in space."

As if to punctuate that, one of the consoles behind them sizzled and exploded in a shower of sparks. "And because we can't meet them, so might the *Enterprise* be."

Chapter Eight

U.S.S. Enterprise, NCC-1701-E
Romulan space
Sector 142

Two days ago

"WE HAVE A PROBLEM." Beverly Crusher walked into Picard's ready room in a manner that could certainly be considered a barge.

"That's not what I wanted to hear."

Beverly looked tired, and Picard knew how she felt. He'd not really slept in days. Sure, he'd tried, he'd pretended by changing into bedclothes and turning off the cabin lights . . . but whether he'd actually slept or not was open to interpretation.

"Kalor is dying," she told him. "Slowly but surely. The blood loss for him is too much."

Picard sighed and his chest felt tight, a rock of tension weaving its way between his ribs. "I thought you were filtering his blood but he wasn't losing anything."

"Something is always lost in the process, and after thirty-nine hours, it's having a detrimental effect." The doctor turned one of Picard's desk chairs toward her and slumped down into the seat.

"Can't you give him something to increase his own blood production?"

Beverly sighed in a manner Picard was used to hearing when he deigned to voice medical opinions. "Not in his weakened condition," she said. "In three hours I'll run out of our Klingon blood stores."

"You need a donor," Picard offered.

She nodded. "And everyone on Kalor's ships has been exposed to a strain of that virus before. To use them as donors in this case would tax Kalor's immune system and could bring *that* strain of the virus out of its remission."

"You mean they didn't cure it?"

"They only stopped it." She leaned on his desk with one elbow, using her palm to support her chin. "Viruses are rarely cured in and of themselves. We can create a vaccine, find a treatment . . . make it so the virus doesn't affect a patient in its remissive state . . . but rarely find a real cure. That's the case with Kalor. And in his weakened state his virus could reassert itself."

Picard nodded solemnly. "What you need is a Klingon who never was exposed to that virus, in any form."

"Yes."

The captain stood. "I think I know where to find one."

Lotre sat in the command chair of the *U.S.S. Enterprise,* letting his useless disruptor rifle balance back and forth as one finger cradled the trigger guard.

He'd lost his men hours ago, and he'd lost his anger sometime after that. He sat now in what he knew to be a fake captain's chair, staring at a fake viewscreen, wallowing in his all-too-real failure.

When the fore turbolift door opened, Lotre was only mildly surprised. When Jean-Luc Picard, the man Lotre had "killed," entered, he was even less so.

"Command isn't all it's cracked up to be, is it?" Picard asked, marching toward the Klingon, his phaser raised and aimed.

"I see you're witty, as well as clever." Lotre looked down at his weapon. "No point in aiming this at you, I assume." He tossed it to the deck.

The Earther glanced at the weapon, but didn't lower his own. "No. The moment we beamed you into the holodeck those were useless, except as props."

Lotre nodded slowly and rearranged himself in the command chair. "I should have known," he said. "I should have figured it out sooner."

"Knowing would not have helped you," Picard offered, but there was no accommodation in his voice. Not quite a taunt, either, but more than just an idle comment.

"I suppose not," Lotre said, looking down at his weapon, wishing it were real. "Where are my men?"

Picard moved easily around the arc of the fore

bridge, as obviously comfortable with the lay of the false ship as he surely was with the real one. "Like you, they're stranded in various parts of this holodeck. Each time one entered a room alone, the program sealed him in."

"Very impressive." And Lotre *was* impressed. Picard's trap was elegant in its way, but so frustrating and disappointing . . . and it had caused Lotre to fail T'sart.

"You seem to have killed everyone," Picard said, glancing around the bridge, seeing none of the holographic crew in their positions.

"Only once I knew they weren't real," Lotre said. "My intention was never to kill your crew."

"No, that was something special you intended only for me," Picard barked.

Lotre shrugged. "Had 'you' not been so difficult to subdue."

Picard smirked. "Yes, well . . ." Picard didn't continue his thought, if he had one, and Lotre didn't prod him for more information.

"I'm curious . . . Lotre, isn't it?"

"Yes." Why was he here, Lotre wondered. What did the man want?

"Why are you working for T'sart?"

The question took Lotre by surprise. What did it matter to Picard? He searched the Terran's eyes, looking for satisfying answers. Finding none, Lotre decided to answer honestly. "I believe in him," he said.

Picard shook his head and chuckled.

"You find that amusing?" Lotre felt a twinge of anger in his gut, but he let it roll around rather than release it.

"No, just naive."

His eyelid twitching, Lotre thought that ball of out-rage that was churning his stomach might burst. "I thought you came here to gloat, not insult me."

"You don't think I came here to kill you?" Picard asked and motioned toward the Klingon with his phaser.

"The Federation?" Suddenly Lotre's anger melted and he laughed—slightly at first, then heartily. "I wouldn't be surprised if you came here to offer me tea."

Picard seemed to ignore Lotre's sudden bout of cheer. "How does a Klingon end up believing in a Romulan?"

This caught Lotre and cut him. His chuckle died and he glared at Picard. "I thought the Federation was be-yond racism."

"My apology." The Earther bowed his head.

Lotre snickered darkly. He didn't like Picard, and not merely because he was his enemy. He didn't like his manner and his smugness and he especially didn't like his apology, which was probably sincere and so ruined Lotre's total disrespect for him. It was difficult to have complete disdain for someone who sincerely apolo-gized. But, perhaps Lotre could yet use that. Picard had weakness, and weakness could always be used to an enemy's advantage. "Is this when we order the tea?"

"No," Picard said, and then ordered the holodeck to create an exit. "This is when you save T'sart's life." The captain motioned for Lotre to rise and move to-ward the real *Enterprise* corridor. "And after that, should we all survive, you can stand trial for a variety of crimes."

Chapter Nine

Romulan Warbird *Makluan*
Romulan-claimed space
Just outside the Caltiskan system

Yesterday

"THIS ISN'T POSSIBLE." Folan turned away from the science station scanners, and tried to wipe the expression of what must have been horror from her face. She spun toward the helm. "Full stop!"

The helm officer responded and Medric turned from his own station. "A dead zone around the entire Caltiskan system?"

She shook her head. "No, it's not the same. A dead zone should not show any sensor data—as if looking into a void because the scanning signals cannot make the return voyage." She tapped a few commands into the board to her side and a graph appeared on an overhead monitor. "This is scattered data, a mass of signals that are meaningless." She compared again what the system should look like—one star, six planets, next to another system very close by, a black hole at its center. That in itself was significant.

Folan turned back toward the bridge and found the crew watching her. It struck her how different their demeanor was from just two days ago.

Of course, Medric was the reason for that. She glanced down at the ring on her finger—the same one worn by the attacker Medric had kept from killing her. "He gave me this?" she'd asked Medric when he gave it to her.

"It's all we were able to find of him. He's disappeared. You should probably wear it," Medric had told her. "Prominently."

His meaning was obvious to her, and would be to others as well: don't cross Folan, or one morning you'll wake up dead.

And of course her attacker was dead—who could wind up missing on a starship?

Whatever else Medric did or said to others, Folan could not know, but the result was plain: where once she reaped scorn and disdain, now she commanded respect.

"What are your orders," Medric asked.

Unsure, Folan tried to consider her options quickly. How could she order her ship to fly blindly into . . . well, she didn't know what.

Of course . . . what were her alternatives?

"Ahead," she ordered. "Slow."

The helmsman nodded, Medric nodded, and the bridge crew seemed assured under her command. If only she felt the same.

Folan needed to have the confidence in herself that her crew now had. The problem was she didn't really think they had confidence in her. What they had was fear. While no one publicly spoke of the Tal Shiar, the organization had its roots throughout all Romulan society. That had never been so evident as when Medric was able to secure spare parts from any ship they'd happened to encounter on their voyage to the Caltiskan system. At first anyone they met was most reticent to offer help. A short, private discussion with Medric changed that dramatically.

Now the warbird was almost completely repaired, and under Folan's command. It felt odd to her, less rushed and hectic. It was one thing to take command in an emergency, and there still *was* an emergency, but it hadn't felt that way. The ship was calmer, the personalities more defused. She tasted the power of the Tal Shiar, and liked it, but worried that it was more fleeting than the true respect that came with experience and accomplishment, rather than threats and fright.

She had to prove herself, Folan decided, and as the *Makluan* entered the perimeter of the Caltiskan system, the sensors cleared and she saw her opportunity.

The main viewscreen had shown the visual interpretation of Folan's sensor data: a whitish mass of signals and pulses that made little sense and had no pattern. But as her warbird passed into the area, the sensors and screen cleared.

A surreal swipe of space fell before them. The

starfield looked muted, distorted, and in the lower right corner of the screen a bright flux of space spasmed around another warbird.

Folan stepped down to the command chair. "Magnify that," she ordered, indicating that corner of the viewscreen.

"Yes, Sub-Commander."

The screen flickered, wavered, and when it should have focused on the warbird in the distance, it seemed unable.

"Clear that."

"I'm unable, Sub-Commander."

Folan frowned and strained to understand the scene. There was a spherical object, as big as a starbase, in the center of the screen. The warbird was not too close to it, and at time seemed to be trying to veer away from the object. Then it would tack toward it, and away again. The Romulan starship moved up, down, and around and away and back and . . . it seemed to be caught in a whirlwind of spatial disruption. At first.

And then Folan retreated back to the upper deck and science station. The other warbird, Folan discovered, through hazy and garbled sensor data, was not moving of its own accord. Space was. Or seemed to be. Or . . . she wasn't sure what.

"This is . . . this can't be happening."

"What," Medric asked, and was suddenly at her side. "What is it?"

"That is what I'd like to know." Folan turned to him fully. "I need to know all you know about this, and I need to know now."

"Sub-Commander, I'm getting an erratic sensor lock on the sister ship," one of the operations people called.

"Transfer to my station," Folan ordered, and she twisted toward her computer console.

The data was confusing, and yet in a way made some sense as well. "These energy patterns . . . they're entirely unknown."

Folan looked back to the main viewer and watched the warbird caught in a vortex of space displacement that—

That was it—space displacement or . . . something like it. The warbird wasn't moving that much. Not of its own power. Space around it was, and was taking the vessel with it.

"This is extraordinary," Folan told Medric, excitedly. She was exhilarated and yet also fearful. She wanted to investigate it all, pore over it for hours and hours. "Look at this—that ship is literally in, I don't even know a name for it. Spatial flux, perhaps."

Medric looked at the data. "I don't understand."

"I don't even have time to explain it," Folan said, tucked over her sensors. "That ship is losing structural integrity."

Back down to the command chair, Folan ordered a slow intercept course. And Medric followed her closely.

"What are you going to do?" he whispered. He'd been much more cautious with voicing his concern or disagreement since "the change," when he'd told her she was going to become a member of the Tal Shiar. He'd shown her respect—devotion, even. She even felt in the two short days that they'd perhaps grown into a small friendship of sorts.

"I'm going to get that ship out of there," Folan told him.

The concern that played out on Medric's expression seemed multifold. "You—you said it was the space around the ship, not the ship itself."

"Something like that, yes."

Medric hesitated, then whispered again, very low, "I think this is something we should clear with . . . superiors."

Only now did Folan wonder if Medric had made it clear to others that he was Tal Shiar too. Perhaps not. Perhaps he'd spread rumors about himself, but claimed or hinted only that he was her operative.

It didn't matter. For the first time in two days she felt she could be of some use. "You try and raise them," Folan told Medric and then indicated the warbird on the viewscreen. "And I'll try and save *them.*"

She could tell by the look on his face that he was nervous. What had he said two days ago? Something about the sponsors of Tal Shiar initiates . . . that if the initiate refused, or failed to pass the proper loyalty tests, the sponsor's life was forfeit. Folan was probably on Tal Shiar probation, and not only her neck but Medric's was in the noose if she played *anything* wrong.

While that was a concern, it had to take a backseat to saving the lives of her comrades if she could.

"I will remind you this isn't your place. We don't know what the planners will—"

He was whispering so low that Folan had to strain to hear him and she was looking down, trying not to be distracted by other sights and sounds. But when Medric stopped suddenly, Folan looked up and found him staring at the screen, awestruck.

She followed his gaze and so also watched in awe . . . the warbird in the distance was twisting and turning—the entire ship—as if it were some child's pull toy that could be bent and bowed in the turns of small hands.

"Sensor distortion?" Medric asked breathlessly, but he probably feared the answer.

Folan glanced down at one of the small monitors near the command chair, just to be sure. She shook her head slowly. "No . . . none."

"We can't go—into that," Medric said.

For too long a moment Folan said nothing, then finally, "Tractor beam? Can we pull that ship out of there?"

"Sub-Commander . . ." The helmsman turned from his controls. "I cannot get a tractor lock, or a navigational lock, or—"

"What is it, Centurion," Folan prompted.

The man looked up at her, ashen. "Sub-Commander, I cannot be sure there is space there at all."

Chapter Ten

OF COURSE THERE WAS SPACE THERE. Space was every-where. Wasn't it?

Folan wondered. She'd seen the sensor data herself. It was more gibberish. It was meaningless, and told her there was no *there* there.

No wonder, she thought ironically, the other ship couldn't escape. How does one escape from nowhere?

"Commander, our sensors are overloading," called one of the younger officers who manned Folan's own science station when she was in the command chair.

"Shut down active sensors," she ordered.

"Shut down?" At first Medric's voice was loud and opposing, but he caught himself and rather than making a scene he stepped from his station down to the center seat. "We'll be blind," he whispered somewhat harshly.

Whatever it was that pushed her within herself to be

in command—anger, or hate, or lust for power—she wasn't sure what it was at first, but suddenly it felt like responsibility. To her crew, and to the position. "We'll be blind when the sensors burn out if we don't shut them down." She looked away from him and toward the main viewer—a tacit dismissal of not just his complaint, but of him. "Passive sensors will have to do."

She didn't explain, and shouldn't have needed to, that active scans were doing very little good and Folan saw no reason to burn out circuits that were currently useless to her.

When Medric didn't immediately return to his station, she turned to him and ordered it.

He nodded once, and did so.

"Centurion," Folan said to the woman at the engineering console. "Report."

"Structural integrity is down twenty-three percent."

At this, Medric began another move down to the command chair, but Folan heard him stir and so she spun around and stopped him with a glare.

"Sub-Commander," he said after a moment. "I respectfully suggest we should back away. Our . . . the leadership on the planet—"

She shook her head and swiveled slowly to the engineer. "Can you get a reading of the other ship's structural integrity?"

"I cannot. But from our last good scan, we know it's not strong."

Folan nodded. "And probably getting weaker."

"As are we," Medric added, and while it almost seemed he was back to his old self, there was a difference in his tone from before. His tone was less defiant and more plaintive.

She didn't have time to listen to either. Instead, she went to her old science station and added up what data she did have . . . and then guessed at what she didn't. She remembered a theoretical formula from her training. Something about which scientists speculated and discussed, but the power necessary to prove it beyond doubt was out of reach even of a civilization that could harness the power of suns.

"It's higher-dimensional," she said more to herself than any of the bridge officers. "The problem isn't that there's no space there, but that there is too much space there."

"Too much?" The question might have been from Medric but she wasn't listening very closely.

Rather, she was more interested in the simulations she was running. "Yes, too much. Trust me on this."

"How can there be more space?" This time there was no doubt it was Medric asking. His voice brought her from her self-induced semi-trance and she looked up at him.

"I don't have time to explain theoretical physics to you," she said, trying to maintain a kind, if harried, tone. "We need to send a warp probe into that . . . mess," she told the engineer.

She bent over her controls. "Configuring now."

Folan nodded and tapped at her own computer. "Use this matter-antimatter intermix."

"Yes, Sub-Commander."

In a few moments it was ready, and Folan ordered the probe launched. The warbird spat the mass of sensors forward and then the probe leapt into a flash of warp.

"Commander, telemetry is garbled. I cannot keep a reading."

Watching as the probe sped toward the other warbird, Folan tried to check the telemetry data herself. "Garbled" was understatement. The probe was winking in and out.

"What's happening?" Folan asked. "Did the probe lose power?"

"The probe is . . ." The engineering centurion hesitated, perhaps unsure.

Folan sympathized. She wasn't sure of much, herself. "Report," she prodded.

"I believe it has fallen out of warp."

Nodding knowingly, as if that was just one more piece of the puzzle, Folan ran yet another simulation through her computer. "The warp field collapsed," she mumbled. "That's why the warbird cannot escape. They can't generate a warp field."

Suddenly she noticed Medric was at her side. "What do you propose?" he asked her.

"Rescue them," she answered. "We'll need to pull it into our warp field."

"We can't do that from here."

She shook her head ruefully. "No, we can't." Rising past him, she made her way down to the command chair. "We've got to go in there."

Medric's face soured. He was making it very clear he didn't like this course of action.

Having switched some of the basic controls of the science station to the center seat, Folan checked the murky data on her monitor. "We need them to stop. Can we hail them?" she asked the comm officer.

"I've been trying for some time," he said. "There is too much interference."

Folan nodded. "Weapons officer, bring disruptors online. Can we target their sublight engines?"

Stunned silence trampled the bridge.

"You want to fire on one of the Praetor's ships, ma'am?" asked the weapons officer, the young man's eyes wide with probably both fear and surprise.

"Yes," she snapped at him. "And we must hurry. Can we get a weapons lock?"

Still taken aback, the centurion checked his board. "Uh . . . I can lock for *when* we fire, but to our perspective the ship is moving instantly from one place to another, around and around. I don't know that we can confirm contact."

"It's possible," Folan said, "that our fire will follow our sister ship on its odd trek—*if* we can angle it right."

If the bridge had been tense before, it was ten times that after she'd given the order to fire on another Romulan vessel. Orders were fuzzy on this point for any crew. They were to remain loyal to their commander until the bitter end, and if they did not, their bitter end might come sooner than they'd hoped. By the same token, they were to remain loyal to the empire as well, and in just the same way.

Once again, Medric was at her side. He'd been zipping up and down so often that Folan was ready to have him restrained into his seat.

"Pardon my saying so," he whispered, or perhaps spat quietly, "but are you insane?"

She looked up at him, his fiery, angry eyes, and wondered herself. She was begging for death. "There's a duty—" she tried to explain.

"But if you fail—" he hissed.

"I *won't* fail," she whistled past the graveyard.

"If you do," Medric said, leaning into ear, "we're both dead."

"If I do, everyone on this ship, and everyone on the other ship, is dead already."

Folan turned away and Medric's retort never came, though she thought she might have heard him audibly gulp.

"Sub-Commander, I might have a lock now."

Pulling in a sigh, but trying to make it sound more like a deep breath, Folan almost decided against this path. Maybe she should seek orders first.

And then she saw the other ship's structural-integrity reading again. This was what command was all about, and in making this decision she was proving that to herself, if no one else.

"Fire."

Bright green lances of energy plunged out from the *Makluan* and into the disjointed space before them.

They didn't connect with the other warbird, and instead became bouncing parallel lines that danced one way and then another, dislocating themselves in a mess of power that eventually dissipated.

"Again, fire," Folan ordered.

And again, the result was the same.

"It's not working," Medric said.

Folan shook her head and tightened her fingers on the arms of her chair. "Again."

Raw power forcing itself forward, more disruptor shots pierced into the mosh of disrupted space. Once more they boomeranged hither and yon until disappearing into oblivion.

Cramming her eyes shut, Folan repeated her command. "Again!"

Another dance of energy and light, but this time, followed by a gasp. Folan blinked and there was a clash of debris and electrical flame cradling the trapped warbird.

"That's it!" She spun toward Medric. "Are they stopped?"

"I—I believe so. They are slowing."

"We'll need to act fast." Folan found herself standing, bouncing on the balls of her feet. "Medric, be ready to extend our warp field."

"We'll require a completely different field matrix."

She leaned down and punched commands into the arm of her command chair. "I'm sending it to your console now." She tapped more keys. "Helm, plot this course." She wasn't used to giving all the command— she found herself doing half the work herself.

"Plotted."

"This will take us right to them?" Medric asked the helmsman.

"I'm not sure. I hope so."

"Stand by on tractor beam," Folan ordered. "Lock at point blank." She was bouncing again and tried to slow herself, if not stop altogether. "We can't slow down to verify a true sensor lock. I don't even know if a sensor lock would work."

Lowering herself into the command chair again, Folan shared a glance with Medric. His eyes broadcast his thoughts: *I hope you know what you're doing,* they said.

So did she.

"Engage."

Chapter Eleven

Private vessel *Loa-var*
Romulan space
Sector 101

"WE'VE WASTED A LOT OF TIME," Riker said, mostly to himself. He was irritated by circumstance and feeling useless without a specific task on Tobin's small bridge.

When the "dead zone" turned out to be only a few burned-out power relays, there wasn't much time to celebrate. Riker knew they'd missed the rendezvous with Picard, and so he'd opted to not even attempt the meeting. If alive, *Enterprise* would have been on their way to the Caltiskan system by now—so that was where Riker was headed.

Tobin's small bridge shuddered.

"What was that?" Tobin asked.

"Subspace shear," Data said, turning away from the scanner console and toward Riker. "Another spatial disruption, sir. Not a dead zone, but perhaps related."

Riker nodded, and noted Tobin's worried glance. The Romulan had been very quiet on their journey. He'd stopped complaining, and even spoke briefly of Nien's courage, and how it had inspired his own. This wasn't what Tobin had expected at all, and Riker had offered to find an M-class planet to leave him on, reminding the Romulan that their mission now meant almost certain death.

"As I understand it," Tobin had said, "if you do not succeed, that will be my fate sooner or later."

He was right, of course. As the ship quaked around them again, pushed beyond its limits for hour upon hour, Riker wondered just how soon that fate would come.

U.S.S. Enterprise, NCC 1701-E
Romulan space
Sector 142

"I don't know which sickens me more—that you work for such as him, or that your cowardly blood mingles with my own." Kalor's voice was weak, his bravado the façade a dying man might show both his enemy and his family.

Lotre was not his family. "A coward is someone who chooses his own path?" he asked, from the biobed next to Kalor's. The two Klingons were attached at a contraption that pulled blood from one, filtered it, and gave it to the other.

"A coward is someone who works for a murderer," Kalor spat, probably using too much energy on a useless argument he could not win.

Lotre was content to continue the debate, however, and let his opponent weaken himself more. "Of course, the Klingon heroes you worship never murdered anyone," he offered sarcastically.

His hair rustling against his bed pillow as he shook his head, Kalor rasped, "You'd side with him—against your own people?"

At this Lotre bristled. "The Romulans are my people. I was raised Romulan, and I live Romulan."

Kalor seemed to attempt a chuckle, but it sounded more a cough. "And they accept you?" he asked facetiously. "They don't fear you?"

"They do not fear me."

"Liar," Kalor said.

Such a charge stung, because it was somewhat true. There was no way to hide his genetic heritage, short of reconstructive surgery, and his parents had taught him that shouldn't be necessary. Adopted as a war orphan on a Klingon colony seized by Romulans, Lotre had very loving Romulan parents. He didn't remember any Klingon relatives, and didn't care to. On his own he rejected Klingon culture, and had always been satisfied with that decision. Most Klingons he'd met had not.

That was, perhaps, a large part of his loyalty to T'sart. T'sart was one of those Romulans who saw Lotre as an individual, not a member of a genetic group.

"I am saving your life," Lotre said finally, and knew

his silence had acted as acknowledgment. "So why don't you just be silent and take the charity?"

"You save my life only to save his." Kalor shifted, seemingly uncomfortable in his biobed. "You'd kill me as soon as look at me, otherwise." He then mumbled something so quietly that Lotre had to strain to hear it: "And I have been ready to die since my planet was lost."

"That is the difference between us, Klingon," Lotre said, using Kalor's race—and his own—as an insult. "You would kill, but I would not. I can control my passions. I am a Romulan."

"You're a mongrel like anyone. You lie to me, you lie to yourself, you lie to your blood. But your blood does not lie to me. I hear it, and it wants to kill me."

Lotre sighed. Typical meaningless bravado. "If my blood wants anything, it merely wants you to shut up."

"Very glib, *brother,* but racked with denial."

"You're delirious." The osmatic suction on his forearm was itching again, as it seemed to periodically, and he thought about calling the nurse. It would be gone again soon, and he decided against it.

Kalor smiled, and from their horizontal angles and in the dim light, he looked rather demonic. "I'm delirious because I suggest deep down you're truly loyal to your own? You should take it as a compliment."

"I *am* loyal to my own. I am a Rom—"

"Stop! I will not hear this!" Kalor rasped angrily and became suddenly animated, pushing himself up on his elbows. "If true you are an abomination! You are a cancer who dilutes his race by choosing water over blood!"

Lotre couldn't resist the chance to bait Kalor further. "No. In fact, water is thicker than blood."

"Your skull is thicker than anything."

And then, as if deciding after a long moment, Kalor lunged off his bed and fell on the deck, pulling down the intricate equipment between himself and T'sart, as well as between him and Lotre.

Looking down on the Klingon with more shock than anything, Lotre felt unusually strong fingers clamping his ankle and pulling him down to the deck as well.

They wrestled there, grunting in weak combat. Well, Kalor was weak anyway. Lotre could have killed him, and his hands had even found the Klingon governor's throat at one point. But he refrained. He would not become that which Kalor demanded he was. But it would have been so easy, and as he gritted his teeth and anger welled in him as well, he *did* want to express it physically. He did—

Alarms were going off—the disruption of the medical equipment—

Someone sedated him—he felt the hypospray on his neck, heard the hiss.

"He tried to kill me," Lotre said weakly.

Through the fuzz of tenuous consciousness, Lotre heard some human woman say, "I'm only surprised it took this long."

Sleep came quickly, coaxed by drugs and fatigue and the sheer accomplishment of goading Kalor into acting like the animal he was.

But when he realized he was sleeping, he forced

himself out, pushing back the darkness as he squinted into the probably still dim sickbay light.

"T'sart?" he whispered across Kalor's bed.

"Is the dog curled up and sleeping?" T'sart asked.

Lotre smiled. "Yes."

"Good. Come where I can see you."

Gently guiding the tubes that connected him to Kalor, Lotre navigated around the biobed and stood at T'sart's side.

"I have failed."

"Yes," T'sart said lightly. "You have."

"There are no words for my sorrow." Lotre didn't feel he could look his friend in the eyes. Not only for his lackluster performance in taking over the *Enterprise,* but because it pained him to see T'sart so ill. The man was a second father to him. He would not see him die for anything.

"You shall redeem yourself, my son." T'sart reached up and clasped his arm strongly. "I am in better health than one might think," he whispered, ". . . and we will make plans."

"He's not as sick as he wants us to think." Beverly Crusher dropped the data padd on Picard's desk and huffed as she lowered herself tiredly into one of his ready-room chairs.

"I imagined that might be the case." Picard swiveled the padd toward himself, glanced at it, then pushed it toward Spock, who sat in the chair next to Crusher's. "He's planning something," the captain said.

"Why are we letting him talk to Lotre—someone he can plot with?"

"There are guards present," Spock said.

"But not within earshot," Crusher pointed out. Her eyes were a bit sunken. She'd been up how long, taking care of Kalor and T'sart, and now Lotre?

"They're being listened to, Doctor," Picard assured her. "But they're far too smart to speak forthrightly alone, let alone in anyone's presence. When they talk, it will likely be in a preplanned code."

"How can you be sure of that?" she asked.

Picard glanced at Spock, who seemed to shrug without really doing so. "It's what I would do," Picard said finally.

By the look on Crusher's face, the captain thought that only rank and respect was keeping her from rolling her eyes.

"Thank you for your report, Doctor," Picard said, motioning to the padd still in Spock's hand. "What about Kalor?"

"We've had to restrain him," she said. "He tried to kill Lotre."

"Talk about biting the hand . . ." Picard murmured.

Eyebrows arched in annoyance, Crusher nodded her agreement. "Kalor is weaker for the struggle, but no great harm was done. Lotre is strong and neither that nor the transfusion is affecting him much."

With a crisp nod and a grunt, Picard asked, "Exactly how well is T'sart?"

"Virus levels are down to seventeen percent," she said. "Pretty well, I'd say."

Spock laid the padd gently on the desk. "He will attempt another takeover."

"From sickbay?" Crusher asked, her brows furrowed.

The captain leaned back in his chair and sighed in a manner he thought not very captainly and would not have allowed himself on the bridge. "Perhaps." He motioned toward the door. "Get some rest, Doctor. We're all going to need it."

Crusher nodded, rose, and walked smoothly out the ready-room door.

As soon as she was gone, Picard turned to Spock. "We need to talk."

The Vulcan nodded. "So I surmised."

Rising, Picard walked to one of his office windows. He picked a star and followed it from foreground and into the distance. "I can't trust T'sart, now more than ever."

"Less than ever," Spock corrected.

Picard chuckled. "Yes. I'm tired myself."

"A common grammatical error," Spock said.

The captain turned back and allowed the Vulcan to see his smile. "Did you correct Captain Kirk's grammar?"

"Rarely."

A difficult man to read, for a human if not a half-Vulcan, Spock was an enigma. He'd lived in a past time of great upheaval, much as Picard and his crew did now. How many times had the fate of the galaxy hinged on what decisions he and Captain James Kirk had made?

"Back to T'sart. I want to assume everything he tells us is a lie."

Only a moment's pause before Spock answered. Picard turned back to see the Vulcan's fingers steepled before him. "I would submit that is an overly broad assertion. There is obviously something to his data and what he says. We've witnessed that firsthand."

"Yes, but we can't trust the details." The captain sat. "We can only trust what we witness ourselves."

"Do you believe our course toward the Caltiskan system is foolhardy?" Spock asked.

A good question. Picard had asked himself that numerous times in the last few days, especially when he was in bed, not sleeping. "No. I think T'sart wanted us there for some reason. Perhaps to stop whatever's happening, perhaps to control it for his own ends. That, in fact, seems more likely. In any case, more than that we can't yet know, nor should we rely on T'sart's word."

"With that I would agree. However, we're approaching the Caltiskan sector. We know something is not right. We're increasingly unable to scan large areas of space. Not dead zones, but odd spatial disruptions that sensors cannot penetrate."

Picard nodded. "I've seen the sensor logs. Astrometrics might as well shut down rather than try to make sense of it all. Have you any idea what kinds of disruptions these are?"

"I would need to be closer in order to investigate."

Well, that was the decision then, Picard thought. "You'll have your chance," he said. "I want you to go in first. You have the unique ability to disguise yourself as a Romulan, better than anyone. And we have your Romulan shuttle, should you be noticed."

"That will need to be repaired," Spock said, his determination to accomplish the mission seemingly instant.

"Already under way."

"Specifics of my mission?" the Vulcan asked as he rose.

Picard pursed his lips. Another good question, and he somewhat fumbled for a non-vague answer. He couldn't come up with one. "See what's out there . . . and report back." He raised his brows in sympathy. "Simple to say, I know."

"Yours is a position of difficult decisions," Spock said.

From the truth of that statement, Picard's thoughts wandered to Riker, Troi, and Data. He'd made a difficult decision just a few days ago, and they had probably paid for that with their lives. Such was a characteristic of command, inherent in the duties to protect the many. Difficult decisions always abound. "This is one of them."

"And a logical one," Spock said, and Picard believed he'd never heard a higher compliment.

Chapter Twelve

Romulan Warbird *Makluan*
Romulan space
Caltiskan system

WHATEVER HAD HAPPENED to the space around them—
in them—it hurt. Folan was having trouble focusing,
and she clutched at her head with both hands, pressing
her fingertips into her skull.

"Get—lock."

"Can't—"

Struggling out of the command chair, Folan stumbled toward the tactical console. "Just—try . . .
blind!" She gave the order to her subordinate, but
pounded the commands into the control board herself.

"Warp field is collapsing," yelped the helmsman.

"Keep it together!" Folan ordered. "Do we have them? Do we—"

"We're pulling them out!" Someone said it, but Folan wasn't sure who. She was looking down, at her boots, at the deck, her brain thrashing about within her skull, begging to explode.

"We've fallen from warp—" Helm again, yelling, barely heard over the din of—what? Folan wasn't sure. It was loud, as if all atoms were singing at once with a strange vibration, off-key. A trillion violins breaking at once inside her head.

She tried to look around, get back to the command chair.

"I can't get sensors online!" Medric called.

The helmsman pounded at his console. "My systems aren't responding! We're out of control."

Folan crammed her eyes shut and wished she could block out all else. But the horrible noise that seemed almost physical bombarded her, and as her bridge crew called out around her, she didn't know who said what anymore.

"Warp power is offline."

"Auxiliary!" she ordered.

"Not responding."

And then it all just stopped. As dust settles after a storm, so Folan's body and mind did. The pain and the cacophony waned and she slowly shook off the agony of whatever had happened. All that was left now was a ringing in her ears and an ache throughout her body.

"Auxiliary power," one of the engineering crewman huffed, "is now responding."

"Sensors?"

Awed by his own response, Medric reported, "Active. Not showing anything, but active."

"The other warbird?" Folan demanded, stepping awkwardly and a bit dizzily toward Medric.

"Off our port." He looked up at her, his continued awe slackening his jaw.

"We did it," the helmsman whispered.

We, Folan noticed. They were one crew, and they now trusted her. Perhaps more than they ever had Commander J'emery.

Her chest still tight and aching, Folan returned to the command chair to rest. She suddenly thought others might be more injured than she. "Casualties?" she finally asked.

"Light, Sub-Commander," Medric said after checking a readout on his console.

Nodding her pleasure, she motioned back to him and noticed her arm was sore too. Everything was sore. "Open a channel to the other ship."

"Trying."

She swiveled back to another centurion. "Secure a tractor beam. Let us tow them to the planet."

"Impressive," Medric whispered, and when she turned back around she found him at her side.

"I wasn't sure it would work," she admitted.

"But it did," he said, smiling widely and bending to her ear, "and you have done very, *very* well."

Medric was not the only impressed Tal Shiar. The high-ranking Tal Shiar at the Caltiskan planet was as well. He'd been a tall, thin, imposing man who held little emotion in his features save for a rather sinister gaze that actually scared Folan as if she were once again a schoolgirl.

She'd thought that returning to the *Makluan* would have made her feel more at ease, but it did not. She saw too much uncertainty on the planet. An alien installation, controlled by Tal Shiar scientists who admitted they knew little more about it now than when they'd arrived.

Lack of sleep cramped her neck and as the lift doors let her onto the bridge, Folan stretched her tight muscles by cocking her head from shoulder to shoulder.

She was too tired, too confused to think about it all.

Medric, who'd apparently not stopped in his quarters on the way back from the transporter room and had made it to the bridge before her, rose from his station as soon as she entered.

"Sub-Commander, sensors are repaired." He handed her a padd. "A list of systems that are not yet repaired, and their estimates."

"Thank you, Centurion."

"What did you think of the installation?" he asked in a hushed tone as he followed her down to the command chair.

"The scientific center on the planet? I've never seen the like. They would not let me view all the data—"

"Oh, in time," he assured her. "In time I'm sure they will. Did you see the accolades given us? Are we not an extraordinary team?"

"I'm a scientist," she said. "It is likely I could help." It was her area of expertise—power and energy consumption and production and conversion. And that was why she felt uneasy at just the hint of data they'd let her see: it hadn't matched their words. "They want to return the sphere to the black hole. I'm not sure that course would be the wisest—" Her voice had been starting to rise and so he cut her off.

"They have the best minds in the Tal Shiar working on this," Medric whispered. "And you have another mission. Destruction of the *Enterprise* and T'sart."

"Surely," she whispered back now, "someone else is more competent to that task."

"That isn't how we work," Medric explained, leaning close, resting his palm on the back of her chair. "The Tal Shiar works through others, rarely overtly on its own behalf."

There was a logic there that escaped Folan, but she did not pursue it with him.

"Are we—is the Tal Shiar—" She looked at him. "Who really has done this? They blamed T'sart for creating the dead zones, but I know he has been with us when those zones were getting increasingly worse."

"T'sart is to blame, of that you can be sure."

When Medric spoke his name, hate filled his eyes as surely as they might her own. Except that she felt now more confusion than hate, and that in itself confused her.

"This all seems . . . too dangerous to toy with," she said finally. "Attempting to return the sphere—"

He turned her chair so she faced him fully. "You're very intelligent, Folan, very bright . . . but know your place."

It was the first time in days that he'd made any

veiled threat to her. And with her newfound respect and power, she didn't like that at all.

U.S.S. Enterprise, NCC 1701-E
Romulan space
Sector 142

"Spock to Enterprise, *on coded channel."* Already the communication was cleaved with static.

"We read you, Mr. Spock." Picard wasn't so much nervous as he was anxious and on edge. Starship captains didn't get nervous. Did they?

"I am two point three million kilometers from the edge of the negative sensor field."

The captain nodded. Normally such information would have been redundant, but sensors were iffy at best, and so Spock was calling out what information he could. "We are keeping an active comm link at all times. You've got one hour, but should you lose it, return immediately."

"Acknowledged. I am entering the field."

After that message, other than a few short bursts of static, there was eerie silence.

Geordi La Forge, at the engineering station, looked forward to Picard and they both exchanged a glance.

"Spock?" the captain finally asked.

"I am here, Captain."

Collectively the *Enterprise* bridge heaved a sigh of relief.

"Nothing to report per se," he continued. *"Sensor readings are ambiguous. I seem to be in a zone of spa-*

tial flux, at least on some levels. My vessel is intact, but structural integrity is being taxed."

Picard inched forward restively in his command chair. "Do you need to return?"

"Negative. I am adjusting power distribution settings. I am, however, scanning an incomplete plastiform patch in my hull. It is spherical and was not damaged in the previous attack by the warbird."

"How can you be sure?" Picard asked, his brows knitting in puzzlement.

"The damage seems to have been caused from the inside out, rather than the outside in."

The captain tapped into the console next to his seat. "Send me your sensor data on that."

Within a moment the information began to scroll past.

"I am proceed—outside the—"

"Spock, we're losing you." Picard twisted toward Chamberlain. "Boost the gain."

"Boosting, sir."

"T'sart was apparently—rect at least in the scope of—this."

In the well of his chest Picard got that "bad feeling" that sometimes was an omen of disaster. "Spock, repeat. We're losing you."

"Vessel—roaching. Extensive spatial—tion."

Bounding toward the main viewer and the blanked-out starscape that was the digital equivalent of confused sensors, Picard nearly yelled, "Spock, you're breaking up. Return immediately."

"Hope you can read m—evasive ac—losing p—"

Picard pivoted again to Chamberlain. "What happened?"

The young lieutenant tapped frantically at his board. "The signal is gone, sir."

"Boost the gain again."

Chamberlain shook his head. "Nothing to boost, sir. It's completely gone."

Chapter Thirteen

**Romulan Warbird *Makluan*
Romulan space
Caltiskan system**

FOLAN DIDN'T HAVE TIME to deal with Medric's disrespectful tone. The helmsman pulled her attention just as his voice had trailed off.

"Sub-Commander—sensors indicate a vessel."

She motioned Medric back to his station with a jerk of her head and then swiveled back toward the bow and the helm.

"Type of vessel?"

Medric shook his head but continued running his console. "I cannot get a good reading."

"Take us out of orbit. Full impulse." She turned to Medric again. "Is the other warbird ready for battle?"

"Not yet."

"Damn. Active sensor sweep," Folan ordered.

Frustration marbled Medric's tone. "Inconclusive. Vessel vector is—the same course we were on."

"It is *Enterprise?*" She slanted toward the viewer as if that would somehow give her better resolution in a field of confused sensor data.

"Inconclusive," Medric said. "I only know it's a vessel of some kind."

"Confirmed," the helmsman added.

Folan's aching spine tensed as she straightened in her seat. "Stand by disruptors."

The helmsman looked down, checked a status screen. "One bank is charged, the other offline." He shook his head. "Not enough against a Federation battle cruiser."

Folan frowned as Medric said, "It will have to do."

"Ten seconds to weapons range," called the helmsman.

With just one disruptor bank and incomplete sensors, this felt like a fool's mission. "I don't suppose we can get a weapons lock."

"Not in this system, ma'am."

"What if it's not the *Enterprise?*" Folan asked Medric across the bridge, perhaps more loudly than was appropiate.

"What other ship could it be?" he asked in return. "I respectfully suggest to the sub-commander that this may be the only chance to strike them hard. Remember, outside the perimeter they cannot scan in. They will not be ready for an attack."

Folan wasn't sure how much discretion she had in her orders. She was very new to the Tal Shiar stratum.

Did Medric outrank her in that system, whereas he did not on her ship? And which overrode what?

"How much of a weapons lock could you get by using navigational rather than tactical sensors?" Folan asked. If she *was* going to do battle with the *Enterprise* she'd rather not be so hobbled.

"Very minimal," the weapons officer said.

"What the devil does that mean?" she snapped.

"Thirty percent accuracy, perhaps."

"Well that's better than firing blind," Medric said.

"Helm, use navigational sensors and try to lock on." She couldn't even see the vessel yet. If they could fire now, with this much surprise advantage, perhaps they'd have a chance to win against the Federation flagship.

"In range, Sub-Commander," Medric said.

She hesitated and he prodded her. "Sub-Commander?"

Trying to ignore the bad feeling she had about it, she finally gave the order. "Fire."

One green disruptor lance sliced out, and from the explosion that flashed on the screen, even though it was distorted by hampered sensors, the charge was a direct hit.

A mass spiraled toward them, out of control.

As soon as it came into clear view, Folan stood in awe. "Praetor's shield! It's a shuttle. A Romulan shuttle!"

The bridge crew gasped. They'd perhaps killed a Romulan citizen.

"Damage report!" she ordered.

"U-us or them?" Medric asked.

"Them! Them!"

He bowed over one sensor console, then another,

working hard with anemic data. "Their hull is compromised."

She pivoted quickly to the engineer. "Transporters?"

He looked desperately sorry for his next words. "Online, but I don't know if we can get a lock."

She waved off the notion. "Just beam any life-forms you find!"

He nodded and pounded quickly into his controls.

As she waited, Folan realized what she had done—and it was the first time for it—if the people in that shuttle died. She'd killed an innocent. Yes, she was a scientist, and yes, she was military as well. She understood war and killing and their necessary role in the universe. But an innocent—someone just minding his own business . . .

"Well?"

"We've got one. If there were more . . . they're dead."

"Medical team to transporter room." She rushed toward the lift door. "Let's hope whoever it is *was* the only one. Medric, with me."

Just as they arrived in the transporter room, two security officers—standard procedure—were escorting the man beamed aboard to a waiting area.

"Scan complete," one of them said, then turned and saluted Folan as he noticed her. "Commander, we've done an identity scan. This man's name is—"

"False." The stately-looking man stepped forward and greeted Folan with a nod. "My real name is Spock."

The name was neither unknown, nor without impact. Both Folan and Medric shared a wide-eyed glance.

Medric was the first to speak, presumably when he

realized he was staring. "Guards, put this Vulcan under arrest." He turned to Folan, smiling. "Your fortune continues to multiply."

She raised a hand and the guards stopped stepping toward the Vulcan. "Hold."

Had Medric not been such a self-controlled undercover agent, he might actually have gasped at Folan's counter order. "You—"

"I said hold, yes."

The guards backed off. Medric twitched, so obviously wanting to summon their return.

"Why would you admit what might secure you a death sentence?" Folan asked Spock, somewhat in awe of the legend she had before her.

"Put simply," Spock said, "because the sentence will be death of the galaxy if we do not act now to end the spatial disruptions originating from this system."

"One doesn't engage in discourse with the enemy," Medric whispered harshly. Folan was becoming more fatigued with that rasp.

"He's one of the greatest scientific minds of this century *and* the last," she snapped.

"He's an enemy alien attempting access to a secret scientific base," Medric said, no longer tempering his tone in soft vocal shades.

She turned from Medric to Spock. "Is that true?"

The Vulcan nodded once. "Yes, it is."

"Guards," Medric called again.

"I said wait!" Folan felt her nostrils flare and a rush of blood making her skin warm and tight with anger.

Again she sought Spock rather than Medric for council. "Are you a threat to my ship, or my command?"

Spock shook his head. "No."

"Surely you won't listen—" Medric tried to interrupt.

"Are you a threat to the Romulan government or Romulan people?" she asked.

"I am not."

She thought on that a moment. "I have your word?"

"You do."

"The myth about Vulcans being unable to lie?" Medric scoffed. "Please tell me you don't believe that."

"No." She sighed and tried to keep her tone level. Partly, she realized, because she wanted Spock to see her as reasonable. "The fact that Vulcans act with honor and logic is enough." She looked to Spock. "Why are you here? Yourself, alone?"

"I came to scan within the area of spatial disruption. I did not expect to be beamed aboard your vessel."

"You came here with Picard?" Medric demanded.

"I did," Spock admitted.

"He can be interrogated later," the centurion said. "I doubt he'll give us useful information without intensive and time-consuming questioning. Since the *Enterprise* is close, and we have perhaps lost the advantage of surprise, I recommend we return to orbit and see to the repair of the other warbird."

"We have a . . . captive from the ship of our enemy and you don't want to interrogate him immediately, no matter how long it takes?" Folan asked.

"We have more pressing needs. I respectfully suggest—"

"I leave you to see to them." Folan waved him off. "Please report to our sister ship and see to the needs of her crew and her captain. Oversee all repairs."

Medric stood unmoving and his expression melted into disbelief. "You're putting me off the ship?"

"I've given you oversight of a pressing need," she said, and had she not been so annoyed with him she might have taken the time to delight in his fluster.

"You need my guidance," he said sharply.

Folan shook her head slowly. "Right now, I need your obedience."

Ponderously, Medric stepped out of the transporter room and toward the shuttle bay. Once he was up the corridor, Folan turned again to her Vulcan guest. "Do you know what's going on?" she asked.

"I have an educated . . . guess." He didn't seem to like his own choice of words. "I was hoping to see your data."

Her data was minimal, she thought, but what little she did know of concerned her. She tried to reassure herself that the glimpses of information the Tal Shiar had shown her were not as cataclysmic as they seemed, and suggested to herself that there must be something more, something she was missing from the picture because she wasn't allowed to know.

If Spock could provide her with that piece of data and quell her fears . . .

"I risk much to give you such courtesy," she told him.

"It is appreciated."

She gestured toward the door and as Spock stepped into the hallway she also motioned for the guards to follow them to the bridge. "What is Picard's plan?" she asked once they were in the turbolift.

"There is no well-structured plan at this point."

Folan shot him a look. She didn't believe that in the least.

"T'sart was supposed to supply information necessary," Spock offered, and Folan interrupted him.

"T'sart," she nearly spat. "You trust him."

"No. But he has provided us with certain information. However, he has also been manipulative and traitorous."

As the lift doors parted, she nodded her acceptance. "That's T'sart."

"Sub-Commander, Medric is on the *S'lar,*" the helmsman informed her.

"Have they finally been able to get above the lower decks there? If so, let me talk to their commander."

The helm officer hesitated, his head lowered. "Their commander is dead."

"Ranking officer?" Folan asked.

"Commander . . . I think you'd better speak with Centurion Medric."

Folan pondered that, and shared an odd and yet somehow familiar glance with Spock.

"Put him through."

Static sizzled across the image as Medric appeared on the main viewer.

Unless she was mistaken, Medric looked pale and scared.

"Medric?" she prodded.

"I—I've never . . ." He stammered—unlike the well-disciplined officer. *"The workers here were just break-*

ing through to the upper decks that had been fused closed as previously reported. We now know why no one had been found below. They all came here. We don't know why. Many of the crew are dead. Most of those have . . . I don't know how to describe it—melded into the bulkheads as if they were beamed into them. Those that remain . . . are insane."

Chapter Fourteen

"WHAT COULD DO THIS?" Sub-Commander Folan sat at the science station of her bridge and pondered the imponderable, with all the great difficulty that implied.

"Many things could," Spock said. "What information have you on this and related phenomena?"

"Just what the Ta—" She caught herself. Not only was she speaking too freely with him, she'd almost told him what could be considered dangerous information for an off-worlder to have.

"The Tal Shiar," he finished. "I am aware of the organization. What have they told you?"

Impeded by pangs of disloyalty, Folan hesitated. How could she really trust him? Solely because he was a scientist she admired? Because he was Vulcan and they were supposed to be honorable? Perhaps she was swayed by his flawless use of the Romulan language?

No, surely not. But whatever the reason, what if Medric was right and to listen to Spock was a mistake?

She'd let her instinct on such matters carry the day before, and doing so had served her well. She decided to do the same again. "That this . . . mechanism, whatever it is, the sphere, has amazing power. Power that T'sart wanted control of. They wanted to stop him from taking it."

"They, meaning the Tal Shiar," Spock said. "And they sought to keep such power for themselves."

She ignored that comment and continued. "This is space-time itself being disrupted. Displacement is larger than I've ever seen. Ever heard of."

"This is what causes the dead zones," Spock said, and though he nearly formed it as a question, she knew he was not looking for an answer from her.

"*We* are the cause, it would seem. Or T'sart was. We are trying to stop it." Folan spoke the words and wondered if she was trying to convince Spock or herself.

"How?" He was talking to her and looking at sensor data at the same time. Amazing, how two races so closely related could be so different in manner. The Vulcans' learned mental discipline was something at which she could marvel.

"I asked how. I asked what specifically was causing this." She motioned to one of the monitors. "That—"

The monitor was a distorted sensor map of a sphere the size of starbase, the mass of a large planet. No other data was listed.

"You are unable to scan within, correct?" Spock asked, as he ran his hands along the computer controls.

He seemed exceedingly familiar with the Romulan control system. Or a very fast learner.

She nodded. "Readings are very garbled. We were lucky to get what cursory information we did."

"It is immense power," Spock said, mostly to himself. "No wonder they all see it as the potential for galactic domination."

"At first I thought T'sart found out about this and sabotaged it. Apparently, he found it, tried to hide it. And when it was taken from him, he tried to destroy it." She motioned with her hand above her, indicating the galaxy in general. "You see the result?"

" 'Found' would seem accurate. He could not have created this, or at least there is no evidence to suggest that he could." The Vulcan seemed to be almost losing himself in his own ideas and theories, and yet Folan mused that he was also probably totally aware of everything going on around him. "He didn't create this, so the question is, who did?"

"I was told it came from the gravity well."

"An object—this massive—being pulled out from, and so obviously surviving, a black hole." He paused, looked at her, and one of his brows drew upward. "Fascinating."

"What could the purpose of this device be?"

"Unknown." Well, the Vulcan was certainly not afraid to admit when he wasn't sure of a fact.

"But it was T'sart's last action with it that created the power deserts."

Spock nodded, and if that was his acceptance of the fact itself, or the fact that she believed it, Folan was not sure.

"I wanted to investigate if that were the case," Folan said. "I asked to see all the data, but those in charge wanted me here, waiting for the *Enterprise.*" She paused, waited for him to look up at her. "What are your thoughts on all this?"

Amazingly, Spock leaned back and intertwined his fingers in thought as he pondered his answer. "This planet," he began finally, "this system—should not be here. Not this close to a black hole."

She needed to think about that only a moment and then the thought struck her and excited her. "Yes! Exactly! That's what I'd been missing. And *that* must have been what drew T'sart to this system. He curried his own forces and took over the science installation on the planet, using superior weaponry to subjugate the populace. And then he killed the science administrator who might have helped him the most."

"I would suggest the installation of which you speak is why this system has been kept from the destruction of the black hole," Spock said.

"So the Tal Shiar scientists think, as well. The planet's inhabitants have the technology to do this, but can be conquered so easily?"

"Since we assume the spherical device, as well as the equipment at the installation perhaps, is unlike the rest of their technology, it is possible they've never studied it enough to duplicate it or learn from it. Look here, and here." He pointed to bits of data on two different screens. "The installation is on the order of several hundred millennia older than the surrounding buildings of this city."

"An ancient civilization's work?" Folan asked. "It does not look like anything we've encountered previously."

"If you'd had, one would assume you'd know better how to use their technology and this might not be a problem at all."

Folan nodded. "And then they could return the sphere into the black hole, and this problem would be over."

"Return it?" Spock's brows shot up in surprise.

"Yes, they've tried, but have been unable." She felt her own brows furrow. "Why? What is wrong? They assume that if this technology on the planet brought it out once, it can do so again."

"If an object of substantial mass enters a black hole, the gravitic and subspace shockwave would serialize this and all surrounding star systems."

She sighed. "I know. They have rigged the proper shielding around this complex. It will survive."

"But the population—" Spock began.

"Yes. They . . . would be forfeit." She frowned deeply. "I don't agree with it," she said. "They've lost three warbirds attempting to get close enough to the sphere to scan it. They have three left, not including this one and the one Medric is working to repair. There's only enough room to pull off the Romulan personnel—" Folan heard how she sounded, and regretted it. Not because she'd been heard, but because she found herself temporizing for values she never used to hold.

"How have they lost those warbirds?" Spock asked, and the question took her by surprise. She expected judgment of her morals, and instead got scientific investigation.

"Spatial forces tear them apart. Each time they do, the disruption of the explosion of the vessel effects the sphere in some way."

"How?"

Folan mostly shrugged. "Long-range scans are very minimally useful. But it is possible that the power deserts coincide with these explosions."

"I'd like to see the data on that."

She punched up a chart to one of the viewers above them. "Here."

With only a minimal glance, Spock seemed to confirm some hypothesis. "Look here, and here."

She read the data, and felt her skin grow clammy.

"This energy wave . . . off the scale. It couldn't—"

Spock nodded. "It likely will. Thrusting this much gravimetric disturbance into the black hole could create a subspace black hole."

"That's so hypothetical—a concept only a few theoretical physicists have even dabbled in." Folan rose and began to pace. "No, no—this isn't possible."

"See the data for yourself." He stood as well and directed her toward the console.

"Praetor's robes—" she breathed.

"A subspace black hole," Spock said, "would pull in matter and energy across dimensional levels, and at faster than maximum warp speed."

She pushed off the controls and began pacing again. She ignored the bridge crew, but likely they were watching her. She didn't care. A subspace black hole was one of the most scary concepts in physics—far more frightening than supernovas and matter-antimatter explosions. If every star in the galactic core exploded at once, the Alpha Quadrant would have time to know it and react. If this black hole became a subspace black hole, then the entire quadrant, perhaps the entire galaxy, could collapse into it in a week's time, with not a ship, not a planet, not a star, escaping its pull. Her mind couldn't wrap around the consequences. "It's . . . how can I even comprehend this?"

"The same way you can comprehend such an object as that being pulled *from* a singularity," Spock offered.

"I . . . I don't know what we should do."

Spock looked down at her. "We should," he said in his deep voice, "proceed using our rational faculties."

Her chest was heavy. "Easier said," Folan sighed, "than done."

"Indeed."

Chapter Fifteen

"IF THE TAL SHIAR SUCCEED, we are all dead." Folan wasn't sure just how loud she'd said that, but as she stopped and looked about the bridge, it was obvious she and Spock were the focus of attention.

"Logic suggests you should act to keep that from happening, if your end is the preservation of life." He was so sure of himself. Philosophical axiom flowed from his lips as water from a fountain.

"I am Tal Shiar myself now," she said as she slumped down into the science station chair.

"And so your moral code has changed? You are no longer seeking life as your valued end?"

She sighed. "What is morality anyway?"

"Morality is a code of values which one forms for the purpose of guiding one's life. You must ask yourself, Folan, what are your values, and why?" He sat down quietly beside her.

"It was a rhetorical question," she said, "but I'll ask you this: How can I choose to betray all that I know?"

The dark orbs of Spock's eyes pressed down on her and held an equal weight with his words. "Choices are only unnecessary when there are no alternatives to action."

"How can there be an alternative to my oath?"

"There are always such alternatives," he told her. "Not having a pleasing choice does not mean your path is without option."

She pressed out a breath and gazed at the image of the sphere on the science monitor until her eyes glazed and began to burn. "Medric's ship and mine . . . we are to destroy the *Enterprise*. If we cannot, the other three warbirds, when they're finished beaming our troops off the planet, will destroy the Caltiskan science installation."

"To what purpose?" Spock asked.

"They fear T'sart will want to access the installation, and that he is working with the Federation," she murmured.

"There is some validity to that notion."

Folan looked up quizzically. "Why let him near it?"

"Captain Picard hopes to control him, and hopes T'sart can bring an end to the dead zones with some ease."

"He is a harbinger of death, not one who would stop such a thing has this. He *does* want to control it. But only to his own ends."

"Of course," Spock conceded easily. "But I have a high degree of trust in Captain Picard and his abilities."

"I have no faith in that man," Folan said. "How can I?"

"I would not ask anyone to indulge in faith. But trusting the data of sense experience is key for any scientist. You must reconcile the facts with your values. I ask you to examine the premises of those values."

She shook her head. "You're asking me to betray my people. How can I do that?"

"I'm asking you to save all people, yours included." Fatherly—in fact, Spock did remind Folan of her father—he gently touched her chin with a finger and lifted her gaze toward him. "How can you not?"

"I—I don't know."

"I believe we are of a mind on this matter," he said, and she felt his words and force of will wash through her.

"You have complicated this matter," she said, and felt such a connection to him that she wondered if she was being a complete fool to have such confidence in him. "I respect you. I am wont to trust you."

He nodded and folded his hands back together behind him. "The situation is grave. Captain Picard will come soon. You must decide."

Never in her wildest imaginings had Folan thought she'd be making such decisions. Even when she took command after J'emery died, she only conceived of having dominion over the most limited determinations. But this . . . where perhaps the fate of the galaxy was ensnared with her next choice . . .

"I'm sorry," she whispered to herself, and stepped down to her command chair. "Address intercraft."

The communications officer nodded and keyed in a code to her console.

Folan pulled in a deep breath and began. "Attention, all hands, all loyal comrades of the empire. This is Sub-Commander Folan. As acting commander of this vessel . . ." She took another breath and then continued. "I am now invoking the Master Dominion Pandect for Martial Crisis. My orders are to be followed completely, and questioned only under penalty of death."

Across the bridge, only Folan and Spock did not gasp, and even Folan thought she might. The gravity of her action, by executing a widely known but rarely used Praetorian mandate, shocked her own sensibilities. It shocked everyone's. But no one would call it treason, as she would legally be obligated to kill them on the spot.

"Stand by on disruptors and torpedoes," she ordered, and the command was followed instantly as she turned to Spock. "We will wait for the *Enterprise,* and protect her from harm with our lives. Should Medric repair his vessel in enough time to join us as he has been ordered, we will . . . do what we must to forestall his attack on your captain's vessel."

"Sir, it's been an hour."

Indeed it had, Picard thought, and quite a long one. "Course plotted?" he asked Rossi.

"Aye, sir."

"Break radio silence. Get me the lead Klingon ship."

Chamberlain nodded. "On screen, sir."

As the main viewer flashed to life, as was his habit, Picard straightened his tunic. "Parl."

"Captain," Parl greeted. "I did not wish to contact you under the communications blackout, but our second ship dropped out of warp for repairs more than seven hours ago. They maintain their cloak, but I fear they will not be able to join us in battle."

Picard frowned. As it was he didn't know into just what situation he was venturing. "I assume that will mean your one ship will fight all the more vigorously."

"Of course." Parl nodded solemnly. "I trust Governor Kalor is well."

"He is recovering on schedule." There was an odd silence where neither man seemed to know what to say, so Picard fell back on procedure. "I will send back a communications buoy in fifteen minutes. Should you not see one, you'll have to try on your own. I'm transferring to you all the data we have, as well as our intentions."

Parl glanced down at something off screen, supposedly a monitor which showed the data transfer. "Understood. We are ready."

"Picard out."

The captain looked out across his bridge. It was his universe, the embodiment of his vision of life. People of all races working of their own wills toward a common goal, building something as pristine and majestic as his ship. And before him lay its destruction, should he not succeed in his mission—a mission the details of which were vague as could be.

No matter—all his other alternatives were invalid. He had to act, and do whatever he could.

"Ahead, one-half impulse."

Comforting vibrations moved through his feet and fingertips as the *Enterprise* pushed itself forward.

Within moments Ensign Rossi reported, "We're entering the null sensor zone."

Geordi moved between consoles at the engineering station. "Power levels are fluctuating . . . no apparent net loss."

"Sensors are stable but reporting meaningless data, sir," Shapiro reported from ops. Data's position. Picard wished the android were there. Regrets had little place in his mind now—they wasted energy and time. He had to push all from his mind but the task at hand.

"Veer off," he ordered. "Take a course separate from Spock's. If someone found him, they may be expecting us to follow his trajectory."

Rossi reacted quickly. "Veering off."

"Come to ten degrees port."

"Ten degrees port, aye."

Enterprise twisted gracefully, then straightened herself.

The captain nodded his approval. "Maintain for two hundred million kilometers, then veer back and through."

"Aye, sir . . . perimeter in ten seconds."

"Shields," Picard ordered, and leaned forward expectantly in his seat.

"As anticipated," said Chamberlain, "shields are nonresponsive."

The choice to proceed was cast and the captain nodded.

"Ahead full."

Chapter Sixteen

IT BEGAN WITH TWO AGAINST ONE.

Chamberlain at tactical: "Two warbirds, 122 mark 15, 125 mark 7."

Picard: "Battle stations! Mr. La Forge, get our shields up."

La Forge from engineering: *"Working on it, Captain!"*

Everyone at their posts. Except Data, Riker, and Troi. And what had become of Spock?

"Evasive pattern theta," Picard ordered, and gripped the arms of his command chair.

"One of the warbirds is vectoring toward us, Captain. They're hailing."

If Picard paused at all, it was but a moment. Still, he was stunned that they wanted to talk. Romulans were generally tight-lipped when they sought their prey.

"Put it through."

The main viewer flashed alive, Spock's static-cracked visage filling the screen. *"Captain, I am well. Sub-Commander Folan has pledged us her help. We will defend your flank, but you must stop the Romulan vessels in orbit of the fourth planet. They seek to destroy an alien installation important to our predicament."*

"Captain," Chamberlain reported, "they are, in fact, firing on the other warbird."

Suppressing a shudder of adrenaline and exuberance, Picard replied with a snapping nod. "Understood. How many ships?"

"Three."

"Well, then the odds are almost even," Picard said dryly.

"I am transmitting what we know. Should they succeed in destroying the installation, the ramifications could destroy the known galaxy."

Picard glanced down, made certain he'd received the data, then pushed himself from the command chair and toward the helm. "Ensign, set a course toward the fourth planet and engage. Ahead full."

"We will attempt—" Spock paused as an explosion shook the warbird and its transmission. *"—resolution at this end."*

"Good luck, Mr. Spock, and my gratitude to Sub-Commander Folan. Yet again."

Folan, standing just to the left of the Vulcan, acknowledged him with a nervous nod.

The captain returned the gesture. "Picard out." He pivoted to Chamberlain. "Tactical?"

The lieutenant shook his blond head. "Hazy, sir."

"Sensors?"

Shapiro dabbed at his console. "Nominal."

Picard marched to the ops console and leaned down over the controls. "Focus the scans. We'll still need a working tactical display." Working together, Picard and the officer swiftly reprogrammed the board and its scanning algorithms.

"It's working, sir."

As the graphic representation of the planet flashed onto the main viewer, the captain returned to the command chair. "Where are the Romulan ships?"

"Must be other side of the planet, sir," Chamberlain offered. "I—Captain, the information the ambassador sent contains better tactical information. Verified it's from Spock, sir."

Shaking his head in astonishment at the Vulcan's skill, Picard breathed, "Well done, Mr. Spock." He motioned toward the main viewer. "On screen."

With Spock's data added to the mix, a grid display of the planet twisted before them. Caltiska IV, class M. Three Romulan warbirds huddled opposite the mass of the planet from them. Without Spock's information, Picard would never have known where they were—sensors were just too impeded by the spatial disruptions in the system.

"Other side of the planet indeed," the captain said. "Any way we approach they'll see us coming far off." He leaned an elbow on the arm of the command chair and stroked his chin thoughtfully with a thumb. Suddenly, he stood. "Picard to engineering. Mr. La Forge, tell me about the shields."

"Firming up, Captain, but we're having problems with—well, space itself, sir. Waves and waves of space-time distortion that make it difficult to configure a stable shield matrix."

Picard nodded and wagged a finger at nothing in particular. "I need them strong enough to withstand taking the *Enterprise* through an atmosphere."

A pause, then: *"Come again, Captain? Tell me you're not thinking of landing the* Enterprise.*"*

"No, Mr. La Forge." Picard smiled inwardly at his own idea. "But we will be flying low."

Sighing, the chief engineer said, *"I'll batten down."*

"Rig for aerial running," Picard ordered as he lowered himself back into the command chair.

"Aye, sir."

The din of orders and status checks, confirmations and reports, filled the bridge.

"Transferring power to structural-integrity fields."

"Forward deflector and fore shields reconfigured."

"Support struts, fore."

"Confirmed."

"Support struts, aft."

"T-fifteen."

"Plate shielding."

"Ninety-seven percent."

"Secure interconnects and confirm."

"Secured . . . confirmed."

To some it might have seemed a garbled mess, but to Picard it was a kind of music that he was somehow able to comprehend. He heard every order—on a certain level—and would know instinctively had something been missing. There was not, however, and his crew was well studied in their duties.

That didn't mean they were without doubt. "Captain?" Chamberlain asked. "If I may, just what are we going to do?"

Picard pursed his lips and felt his muscles tense. Mentally, physically, he was readying for battle. "We're going to surprise them, Mr. Chamberlain. If our ship holds together for it."

Folan could only imagine Medric's surprise and anger—mainly because the first system she was sure to disable on his already damaged warbird was not his weapons or shields, but his communications array. She didn't want him contacting the Tal Shiar command in orbit of the planet. She wanted him silent.

What disturbed her, even as they both battled to disable one another's vessels, was that she hated herself for the decision, and yet knew in her soul it was right. No—that wasn't accurate. Her soul had told her to defend her people. Her mind had shown her the way. The Tal Shiar might have been powerful, and even very smart in the way they manipulated politics and society to their will. But they had a lust for power that corrupted and destroyed, and she knew that the death of the galaxy would be the price of their avarice.

Spock silently worked at the science station as she ran the battle. She'd been a pawn, first of T'sart's, then Medric's, and now this Vulcan's. Perhaps that was when she was most content—following the orders and the rules others set down. And yet, she'd invoked the

Pandect. She decided to dominate by fear: her means justified by Spock's and the Federation's ends.

There was a plasma leak in engineering, and she ordered it fixed. There was an overload in one disruptor bank, and she had power transferred to another. The ship's doctor reported casualties . . . she noted it. She ran the battle, but was numb. Rock on one side, hard place on the other, Folan felt crushed by fate.

She was killing, most surely, Romulans on Medric's ship and on her own. Killing some to save many. Math had been a refuge as a scientist. Now it was a rationalization for an action she couldn't believe she'd taken.

"Sub-Commander," the helmsman called, "spatial disruptions are weakening the shields at an increasing rate. We must try to keep the greatest distance possible from the sphere."

Folan nodded. "Yes, try to lead them away."

At first she liked the battle, when she was filled with rage and hate toward T'sart and Picard. Now she simply wanted it all to end.

And though she knew Spock was right, she wondered what her life would be like should they succeed. Would she be a hero, or an outcast forced to live in an alien culture to avoid execution?

She didn't know . . . and she wondered just how she could win a battle for the life of her ship and the galaxy, when she didn't much care for her own.

Chapter Seventeen

"WE'RE N-NOT S-SUPPOSED t-to be d-d-doing this, y-you know, sir." Geordi La Forge hung on to the bridge engineering console as the *Enterprise* vibrated around him.

On the main viewer, little could be seen past the burning atmosphere as friction against the shields created a fireball that *Enterprise* rode across the planet.

It was a strategy no one could remember anyone having employed. It wouldn't have worked at any normal time, but with sensors bordering on useless, the Romulans wouldn't be looking for—and wouldn't have seen—a Federation starship approaching from on the planet itself.

"S-sometimes," Picard said, through gritted teeth as he too grasped onto what he could for support, "one must b-break a few regulations to make the day, Mr. La Forge."

"A few regs, a few teeth—" Above them a loud creak

went through the upper bridge deck. La Forge eyed the ceiling suspiciously. "A few starships . . ."

Starships were majestic in their looks, aerodynamic in their lines, but that was aesthetics, and usually not for pragmatic purposes. They were held together more with forcefields than rivets and alloy molds. The *Enterprise* could travel in an atmosphere, but she wasn't supposed to fight there—that wasn't her purpose. Today, she must.

Chamberlain stood, nearly hugging the tactical console. "I had a dog who would've loved this—open a p-port and let him stick his head out the window."

"A-at this speed, his head would have ripped off." Rossi at the helm was now getting into it.

"Well, he'd have died happy," Chamberlain said.

Laughing in death's face was one tactic, but this wasn't it. There was, however, after so much time doing so little, an exuberance in doing something active and new. Even if they were not sure success would be the result.

"They s-should be above us now, sir." Despite iron grips to a ship that was trembling around them, Chamberlain and all of them were still doing their jobs.

"Veer straight up, Rossi," Picard ordered, and noted the oddity of the command. "Straight up" didn't really exist in space. But for the next few seconds, they weren't *in* space.

Enterprise smashed through the stratosphere, rending upward until finally she tore up and over the exosphere. She wrenched a tail of burning, bubbling air winding behind her as the sensors cleared—somewhat—and with it the main viewer.

Three warbirds, just where they should be—their underbellies open and waiting. The fight was new.

"Weapons range in five . . ." Chamberlain began the count.

"Shields didn't make it, Captain!" La Forge ducked a shower of sparks that lit up his console and sizzled onto the bridge.

"Three—Target lock unavailable."

Picard's fists tight to his sides, he eyed the warbirds intently, as if he could focus the weapons himself. "Point blank, Mr. Chamberlain, and fire!"

Column after column of hot, orange fire plunged from his ship and into the waiting prey.

First one, then the other, fell away under the force of the phaser blasts. But the third—she moved, swooped around, turning to fire.

Enterprise rocked, disruptor concussions walloping her unshielded hull plates.

"Damage decks two, three, five, nine." La Forge had moved to the secondary engineering console, the primary a charred hulk.

"Damage-control teams." Picard shifted in his seat. "Shields?"

The chief engineer huffed and shook his head. "Snowball's chance, sir."

Gritting his teeth, Picard motioned to Chamberlain. "Tractor beam. Full force."

"Captain?"

"Swing them out of the way, into one another if you can."

Picard had never savored battle, and didn't now—but

it was action, it was moving forward, or at least seeming to, when the last several days had not been.

The lieutenant's hands danced over his tactical console. "Aye, sir."

Spiderwebbed threads of energy entangled the nearest enemy vessel as *Enterprise* sped out of orbit, then back in, tugging the warbird with it as she went.

"Torpedoes, fire!" Picard ordered, and as the orange orbs darted into one ship, then another, finally Chamberlain released the tractor beam and the warbird was sent spinning toward the planet.

"One enemy ship disabled, Captain."

Enemy. This wasn't how it was supposed to be. Peace, so fragile, and he was trying to save it with his weaponry. No—it wasn't the peace he tried to save now, but life itself. There was never any peace without life first.

"The others?" Picard asked, wishing for an active tactical display. He'd know not only how his own ship was doing, but Folan's as well.

"The other two vessels have suffered damage, but are coming around," Chamberlain reported.

Shots and countershots, disruptors against phasers, torpedoes cracking across orbit as the battle waged on.

"We need to protect the installation—keep them busy." Picard found himself stalking the upper bridge, giving orders, watching Chamberlain's tactical board as well as La Forge's engineering console.

Until what he'd been waiting for, what he'd anticipated would happen again, presented itself at the most inopportune moment possible.

"Captain?" Chamberlain called, the slightest panic in his voice. "The alarm is triggered."

"Damn, T'sart," Picard snapped. "He would choose *now!*"

"Don't *you* need a mask?" Lotre asked him.

T'sart smiled and shook his head. "No, this will not affect me in small doses. Romulans and like races would need to absorb it through the skin."

Lotre looked toward the door that led into the corridor, where even now the gas was filling the Starfleeters' lungs with painful death. "Then you—"

"It will take some time to affect me," T'sart said as he pulled the breathing apparatus from one of the medical storage cabinates. "We shall be long gone by then."

Nodding as he took the mask and placed it over his mouth and nose, Lotre surveyed the room. The few medical personnel had been easy to render harmless. A few well-placed blows to their nerve centers and each one went down in moments. Kalor, of course, lay helpless on his bed. He, Lotre imagined, T'sart would save for last.

Indeed, T'sart walked to the unconscious Klingon and whispered close. "I would take the time to kill you with my hands, but I cannot spare it," he said. "Die as they all will, when the poison out there finds its way in here." He turned back to Lotre. "Are you secured?"

"Yes."

The door opened just as Lotre approached it.

No time for him to react, Picard appeared—wearing a mask of his own, phaser in his hand.

Orange light launched, filled his brain, and melted into darkness—and he dissolved with it.

For the first time Picard could remember, T'sart looked genually shocked.

"Did you think I wouldn't know?" The captain moved toward him, his voice angry, yet muffled by the mask.

T'sart said nothing. He backed up a few paces until his back was against one of the biobed consoles.

The ship rattled around them, but only T'sart looked up and around. Picard's eyes were intent and unmoving, burning themselves into the Romulan.

"You're going to tell me what we need to do on the planet, and you're going to tell me now," Picard ground out, stepping closer still.

As if studying the entire situation through Picard's expression, T'sart cocked his head and made the play the captain knew he would. "You've let a special poison into this room, Picard. I assume you've begun pumping it out, but that will take some time. Your mask will only protect you for so long, and all your unconsicious crew members in here are suffocating as we chat."

Picard waited a moment as if considering that, then bent down—his phaser still leveled at T'sart—and pulled Lotre's mask off. "Then so is he." He dropped the Klingon's mask to the deck.

"He—" T'sart's gaze darted from Picard, to Lotre, then back. "You're bluffing," he sneered.

"Am I?" the captain asked. "He'd kill for you, and you won't even give up some warped claim to power for him. What a father you'd have made."

There was a moment of hesitation before T'sart spoke again. Picard could feel it. The man couldn't be totally heartless, could he?

"He would die for me if I asked," T'sart said finally, shifting his weight nervously from one leg to the other. "And even if I didn't. But you're the one killing him now." The Romulan gestured to the slumped Klingon sprawled across the deck. "What of your exalted Starfleet morals?"

"What about them, T'sart?" Picard stalked closer still. "Do you imagine you can manipulate me to be honorable when you are not? Should I give you that advantage?" He motioned wildly with his phaser, his tone crushing from behind his mask. "We're all dead soon, if you don't stop what you began, so why should I care if you die now or two hours from now, or if he does?" He leveled the weapon directly at T'sart's head. "Why not *now?*"

The Romulan licked his dry lips. "You're not serious."

One more step, and the phaser was almost touching T'sart's forehead. "I'm as serious as a dead man."

"What about the gas?"

Picard almost shoved T'sart onto the transporter dais, and once he was there the captain removed his mask and tossed it down. "There is no gas."

"But the people—"

"The corridors are clear because we're at battle stations." As if on cue, a few salvos of torpedoes exploded around the vessel. "I found your little automaton and disabled it hours ago. When you sent it commands, we read them and knew what you were planning. You've been outsmarted, T'sart."

Another explosion, somewhere far belowdecks. Picard wished he was on the bridge, but he knew his priorities well.

"How?" T'sart asked as Picard took to the transporter console, placing his phaser within close reach.

"The hole in Spock's shuttle." The captain began keying coordinates into the controls. "One finely carved incision, from the inside out. Between that and our unexplained damage during the battle with Lotre, it wasn't very hard to figure out."

Picard glanced up and could see that T'sart was seething. He'd been trumped twice, and knew it.

The captain stabbed at his combadge. "Picard to bridge."

"La Forge here, Captain."

"Status?"

"Two to one now, sir. We're making it, but it's slow going. Shields are partially restored."

He looked down at a monitor. "I see that. I need you to take them down for transport."

"Sir?"

"Mr. T'sart and I are going on a very special away mission."

"I just got the shields back up, and you want them down?"

"Afraid so, Commander. I need a security team in transporter room one."

"Aye, sir. On their way."

"Picard out." The captain ran the console controls

162

with one eye on the panel, and one on T'sart. "No more Romulans on the planet," he said. "They'd have been safer there."

"There's nothing to keep them from following you down," T'sart said, his voice filled with outrage.

"Of course there is," Picard said, allowing a smile to curl his lips. "My ship."

The transport was the oddest Picard had ever felt. Space itself was fluctuating, and a transporter beam with it. It itched, almost hurt, but thankfully deposited them in the science installation.

For a moment Picard thought T'sart might lurch away, reach for some hidden weapon, and try to escape. He did not. But he was too somber, too resigned to his fate, and that was worrisome.

Picard motioned with his phaser as the three security guards flanked out to search the room.

"I'll be watching you," Picard told T'sart.

The Romulan sighed out a huff that had it been slightly thicker might have been a hiss. "It's a bit more complicated than flipping a switch from 'broken' to 'fixed.' "

His voice tight, Picard motioned again toward what appeared to be the main console. "Then explain it."

As T'sart began to access systems and change monitors, Picard watched. He'd gotten a glimpse of the city outside the windows, and didn't care to dwell on that vision. The Romulans—T'sart—had laid waste to the nearby metropolis. How many were dead Picard did not know, but he wagered that someone like T'sart would, to the last one killed.

Too long a pause between one and another of T'sart's motions, and Picard asked what was wrong.

"I really think these controls are inadequate to the task," the Romulan said finally.

"You what?" Picard marched toward him, looking at the console. With only a stray look, he certainly couldn't make heads or tails of it.

"My intention," T'sart began with seeming difficulty, "was to use the *Enterprise* to its fullest—its better shields, stronger frame, more complete sensors. We'd had reports the Federation had made certain Borg-inspired enhancements—"

With his free hand Picard gripped T'sart's arm and yanked him close. "You don't have a clue what you're doing, do you? Do you!"

"I do," T'sart insisted, pulling himself away. "I understand this system better than anyone—"

"Which isn't saying much, I gather," Picard barked, his face hot with anger. "You wanted to do what the Tal Shiar wasted time attempting—sending ships in to dissect the sphere with sensors until they knew how to control it. All along you knew little more than they."

"I knew this system was important," T'sart shot back. "A black hole system next to a normal star system with a flourishing world? I knew it shouldn't even be here, and I was the first to form any hypothesis."

Picard shook his head in disgust. "You're a bigger fool than I ever thought." He grabbed T'sart again and pushed him toward the console. "We need to stop this damn thing now."

"If we put it back—" T'sart offered.

"Spock and Folan have already determined what that would do. You'd doom this quadrant, perhaps the whole galaxy, to being sucked into a subspace black hole."

The Romulan waved that notion off with a sweeping hand gesture. "Conjecture."

Picard glared from T'sart to the console, and knew both were useless to him now. "I trust *them* far more than I trust you."

Before T'sart could retort, the captain's communicator sounded with La Forge's voice. "*Enterprise to captain.*"

"Picard here."

"*We can't keep—*" Static scratched the signal. "*—they're firing on the installation—*"

Suddenly, all the controls and computers before them came alive, flashing and almost quaking with activity.

They heard a whine and the security guards brought their weapons up tentatively, cautiously.

Picard motioned them down.

"Shielded," he whispered, then spoke into his combadge. "Mr. La Forge, I don't suppose you should worry about us. This building seems to have its own self-defense system."

"It does." T'sart murmured his surprise.

The captain turned to him and sneered dryly, "I'm astounded at your knowledge of this alien science."

"What the hell is that?" Geordi La Forge nearly fell out of the *Enterprise* command chair, but not because of the disruptor charges walloping the ship. He was staggered by what he saw on the main viewer.

Chamberlain was incredulous himself. "It's a decloaking vessel, sir. Class and configuration unknown. It just rammed one of the warbirds."

"Status?" La Forge asked.

"Warbird is drifting. They've lost propulsion." The lieutenant shook his head. "The other ship is some sort of cargo hauler, sir. And—I—Sir, that ship is trying to beam something onto the bridge."

Leaping from the center seat, Geordi was over the handrail and at tactical. "Can we stop it?"

"Without shields, sir?" Chamberlain shook his head skeptically.

Geordi turned to the lower deck as they heard the familiar hum and saw a flash of sparkle. "I'm guessing we don't have a choice."

A mass of limbs materialized, a lump of . . . people appeared.

Stepping forward, his brow furrowed in surprise and disbelief, Geordi cautiously asked, "Commander Riker?"

Will Riker unwrapped himself from the huddle of people who'd manifested themselves on the *Enterprise* bridge.

"We tried to contact you but you didn't respond," Riker said, looking hot and disheveled. He reached down and helped Deanna to her feet.

"Counselor—" Geordi greeted, still incredulous.

"Only one transporter pad," she explained with a smile. "We had to tear it out of the alcove so we could get here in one beam."

La Forge nodded almost absentmindedly as now his android friend stood. "Data . . ."

"I have never felt so loved," Data said, a small smile

quickly turning serious as the *Enterprise* was racked by disruptor fire.

Data quickly took the ops station and Riker was finding his way to the command chair.

"And who is this?" La Forge asked of the Romulan whom Deanna was helping to one of the free seats.

"I, Tobin," the Romulan exclaimed. "Surrender!"

Deanna took aside, patting his arm. "He doesn't mean that like it sounds," she told Geordi, then turned back to the Romulan. "Your language, Tobin, please."

Tobin took Geordi's hand and shook it as he passed. "Grateful to meet you. I thought we were most certainly dead. Or at the very least, lost."

"I know the feeling," La Forge deadpanned. "We thought you were trapped in a dead zone at the rendezvous."

Tapping orders to damage-control teams into his panel, Riker explained. "We never made it there. We thought we were trapped in a dead zone on the way, but the ship had just lost all power."

"He ordered me to overtax the engines," Tobin added.

"Once we fixed it, we thought you'd gone on, thinking us lost," Riker said. "We knew you were headed here, and the good Mr. Tobin's ship has a cloak."

"Had," Tobin corrected, frowning. He looked up to Deanna. "I will be compensated, yes?"

She smiled. "Yes, I'm sure."

"Status?" Riker ordered.

Geordi shook his head and tried to clear his thoughts. "Right. Captain Picard and T'sart are planetside. Thanks to you, now two of the four enemy Romulan ships in this system are disabled. One is trying to destroy the installation on the planet—"

"With no luck," Chamberlain supplied. "That installation is holding up, with no weakening to its shielding."

"And the other," Geordi continued, "is fighting a fifth Romulan warbird—which is on our side. That's where Ambassador Spock is."

Riker nodded his understanding and Geordi bowed to him. "And now, Commander," he said, more weapons fire sending quakes throughout the ship, "the conn is happily yours."

Moving to the command chair, the first officer thumbed a control on its arm. "Riker to Picard."

Silence bit back at them.

Riker seemed about to call out again, but the turbolift doors parted and two guards, Picard, and T'sart flooded onto the bridge.

"Right here, Number One," the captain said, "and it is good to see you all." He made his way to the command chair, and before he sat down, he glanced at Tobin. "Even you." He turned to Riker. "I'm sure you'll explain all the details later, but for now, we need a plan, and we need Spock."

"What about the installation he said was so important?" Geordi asked.

"I assume it is important. And whomever built it thought so as well—if their automatic defensive shielding is any indication. I doubt a thousand starships could do it harm," Picard said as another explosion crackled against the shields. "Mr. Chamberlain, disable that ship's weapons, please."

"Working on it, sir."

"So who did build it, Captain?"

"That, Mr. Riker, is a very good question, but one we hardly have the time to answer. Assuming we could." The captain looked back toward tactical again. "Mr. Chamberlain?"

"Of the three warbirds in orbit, two are disabled, one is completely dead, sir."

"Life-forms?" Picard asked.

After a moment, Chamberlain met his captain's eyes. "I can't tell, sir. I don't think so."

Sad, Picard thought, but unavoidable. "Rossi, plot a course back to Folan's ship," he ordered. "Let's hope they've not fared as well."

"They're coming around again," the helmsman called. The irritation in his voice was not masked.

Laws could make people act against their will, but no threat or deed could actually *change* that will, and so Folan's crew fought, but not with their hearts, and perhaps only barely with their minds.

"Evasive patterns one, then five," she ordered.

Her shields weak, her weapons failing, Folan wished she'd had the power of a planet at her disposal, just as her original experiment had called for.

Another crush of weapons fire rattled the bridge, sending smoke billowing into the air and insulation dust into the open wound on her cheek. She'd almost forgotten about the wound, but the sizzling pain reminded her, and she looked down at the ceiling support strut that had fallen on her just thirty minutes before.

Spock had said nothing during the battle, he simply sat, meditating with the ship's computer. How he could think with all the commotion . . . he was an amazing man, but his complete single-mindedness also irritated her just a bit. Was he a robot as well?

"Aft shield generators are down."

"Protect our flank," she ordered.

She had to focus, not think of such things and be mindful only of the battle.

"Sub-Commander, we're venting plasma from our port nacelle."

"Damage control?"

"All units are occupied."

So they said. She couldn't

"Warp power is offline."

"Route sublight drive to weapons and shield systems."

"Yes, Sub-Commander."

Spock finally spoke. "Folan, I need to get a message to Captain Picard."

"We lost communications ten minutes ago."

"Where is your communications console?"

She pointed.

"May I?"

"Of—of course."

He moved over to work on it.

"What exactly are you doing?"

"I believe the colloquial phrase would be 'calling the cavalry.' "

Chapter Eighteen

"MR. DATA?" PICARD FELT WARM. Somewhere there was a circuit burning and perhaps a plasma leak. No time now to track them down.

"I am attempting to reroute sensors, sir."

The android probably had no idea how delighted Picard was to see him, to have him working here. Deanna might know, Picard thought, as he glanced at her.

"Counselor, why don't you take Mr. Tobin here to sickbay?"

"Aye, Captain." The woman nodded, her exotic features more angled in the harsh alert lights. She took the Romulan man and escorted him to the turbolift.

"Captain, one of the warbirds from the planet has repaired their propulsion," Chamberlain said. "They are in pursuit."

Picard glanced down at a side viewer and punched

up a gnarled, distorted aft view. There was one warbird limping after them.

"When they're within weapons range," Picard said, "disable them again."

"Aye, sir."

T'sart stepped forward but the two guards who flanked him pulled him back. "Don't you understand, Captain? Your ship has the tools. You will be able to adjust your shield harmonics, your sensors will handle the overloads."

"It's been tried," Picard snapped. "Spock was informed of three Tal Shiar failures. Two vessels destroyed, the other—the crew was either dead or insane."

Struggling against the grip of the security officers, T'sart was pleading. "But you must see they were making progress, the third attempt succeeded—the ship survived!"

"The ship? The ship!" Picard bounded out of his chair, his voice a growl. "It's a thing, T'sart. Do you understand the difference between people and things, lives and materials? Or has your life been about your own personal quest for power, and nothing else?"

T'sart stopped squirming and sneered at Picard. "A man who sits atop a ship so powerful he could carve the stars from the sky, lectures me about power."

"Not power. Morality," Picard said. "You have none."

"Captain, we're receiving a communication," Data reported. "Spock, sir. Audio only."

The captain turned quickly toward the android. "On speakers."

Static scraped and torn, Spock's voice crackled across the bridge. *"Captain, I believe I have a hypothesis worth testing. We must confer immediately."*

"That's the message, sir," Data said.

"Except he's sent more tactical data again," Chamberlain added. "Right to my console."

"Input the data," Picard ordered, then turned to Rossi. "Ahead full."

Her bridge had become a clot of screams, half filled with duty, half with terror as their ship collapsed around them.

"Inertial dampeners are offline!"

A chunk of ceiling debris fell next to the command chair.

"Where are the damage-control teams?"

Sparks showered from a dangling power conduit that spat voltage like an angry snake.

"Commander, we have sustained heavy casualties!"

Someone had died at the engineering station. There was no medic to take him to the medical deck. There was no one to push him out of the way and replace him. Even the doctor was dead.

How bad off was Medric's ship? Was she giving as good as she got? Sensors couldn't tell them.

Folan coughed. Smoke was becoming thick. She'd ordered fans online, but they couldn't cope.

She thought when she was about to die she'd be frightened, but instead she was just very tired. She wanted it to end.

She closed her eyes, heard the whine that must be death, and welcomed it.

Picard and a security guard were marching into the transporter room just as the survivors from the *Makluan* bridge finished materializing. Folan looked confused and surprised. Both she and Spock looked like they'd been through hell—smudged with soot and smoke, hair sweat-caked, eyes having to adjust to the bright room light.

"H-how—" she stammered.

Spock stepped down to Picard and greeted him with an abrupt nod. "Captain."

"Spock, tell me you have a solution." They both began toward the door.

"My ship—" Folan said.

Picard turned back to her as he continued his stride. "Your ship is almost destroyed. Your crew is in one of our cargo bays. But I'd like you to come with us."

Silently, she followed as Picard, Spock, and the guard sped into the hall.

"Spock?" the captain prodded.

"I cannot say with certainty, Captain."

Picard let out a short sigh as all four of them boarded a lift. "Ignore certainty for now, then. What can you say at all?"

"There are two alternatives," Spock began. "Control it or destroy it. Returning it to the black hole, as the Tal Shiar wished to do, is not a viable decision."

"The subspace black hole." Picard nodded. "How do we destroy it?"

Uncharacteristically, Spock hesitated. "I do not know that we can."

As the turbolift moved upward, Picard felt the blood drain from his face. He asked the obvious question, but dreaded the answer. "Then how do we control it?"

"I don't know that we can do that, either," Spock replied gravely.

"This isn't firming into being a very good solution, Mr. Spock," Picard said dryly.

The lift doors opened and they spilled out onto the bridge. "My recommendation is this," Spock said. "We must enter the sphere."

The captain stopped and turned to him. "Mr. Spock, two ships have been destroyed in just attempting to get close enough to scan the object. A third endeavor ended with the vessel's crew either dead and insane. You reported that to us yourself."

Spock said, "I did not say it would be easy, Captain."

Picard huffed out a breath. "You have a gift for understatement, Mr. Spock."

"So I've been told."

They both stepped to the science station, Folan still silently in tow.

"What can we do?" Picard asked.

The Vulcan slid into the station's seat and began using the computer console. "There is a pattern to the disruptions in space-time. We cannot fully attune our sensors and shield harmonics as the adjustments would be too fast for even our computers to handle. But, we can adjust for every sixty-seventh shift."

"Yes, yes, that could work," T'sart interjected from

across the bridge. He was still being held by guards, near the captain's ready room. *"This* is the data I needed—this is the equipment I needed to use."

The Romulan was practically ranting now, lurching forward again. He hated being helpless as his "plan" came to fruition.

Picard was tired of his voice. "Can he help us?" the captain asked, indicating the Romulan with a gesture of his head.

"I would not, at this point, trust any advice he offered," Spock said.

"Get him off my bridge," Picard ordered, nodding to the guards.

Heels dragging as they dragged him into the turbolift, T'sart thrashed about. "No, Captain, I must be present for this. I must! Captain—"

Already turned away as the lift doors closed, Picard leaned down over the science station. "Spock, in order to turn it off, or stop it, or destroy it—"

The Vulcan cut him off. "I do not know the answers to any of your questions, Captain. All I can offer you is this." Spock pointed to a screen above them and an enlarged, computer-enhanced view of a dark patch on one section of the sphere.

"What is it?"

"An orifice," Spock replied. "An opening, leading . . . somewhere."

Picard rubbed his chin. "Somewhere?"

"Presumably the interior of the mechanism."

Continuing to look at the hazy graphic, Picard asked, "Or?"

Spock's head lowered in his version of a shrug. "We cannot know until we're inside. It could be like the inside of a spacedock, or it could be the doorway to another time, another dimension, or another universe altogether."

The captain turned toward Folan. "Do you concur with this?"

She was startled by the question. Apparently she didn't think her expertise was of use, but Picard knew she was a scientist, and to leave her, after her help, waiting in a cargo bay didn't feel right to him.

"I—it seems a . . . logical hypothesis," she said.

Picard offered a wry smile.

"Ensign Rossi, set a course for the sphere."

"Captain, the course has fallen apart. I can't get a heading." Rossi's voice, over the din of what Picard thought must be the sound of hell itself. He squinted through the pain, trying to decipher the voices around him.

"It is the extra-spatial effect, Captain." Spock? He could barely tell.

"Pull back!" Picard looked at Spock and Folan. "Can we compensate?" he croaked out, his own voice was twisted and low, but as *Enterprise* removed itself from the area near the sphere, the whine died and perceptions returned to near normal.

Spock turned to Folan. "You told me you were able to navigate well enough to rescue—"

Booooom!

An explosion pitched the ship to one side and Picard

almost lost his footing. Sprinkles of insulation dust fluttered down and the captain waved them away.

Weapons fire.

"Captain, we're being hailed." That sounded like Chamberlain.

"On screen."

Static played across the viewer as pixels flashed and formed into an angry Romulan visage. "Picard, you are in violation of Romulan—" A sizzle of electric noise disrupted the transmission. "Never mind. Hear this: I will destroy you if you do not pull back now."

"We can stop this, Medric," Folan pleaded, stepping toward the view screen. "Listen to them."

"Traitorous—" Again the connection sputtered and whatever Medric said was lost. "You have her, and you have T'sart, Picard," Medric hissed when the transmission was regained. "But you cannot have this power. Retreat, or be destroyed."

"Captain?" Spock interrupted, and with his look asked for Picard's special attention.

Picard nodded to Chamberlain and had him cut off the comm.

"Our shields," Spock said, "are now specially attuned to the spatial disruptions. We will lose shield cohesion if fired upon."

"Options?" Picard asked.

Chamberlain chuckled darkly. "Throw our warp core at him?"

"Not funny, Fred," La Forge said.

"No, I fear we'll be needing our warp core, but . . ." The captain turned to his first officer. "Number One, we need a one-shot solution to our Medric problem, and detonating a warp core might overwhelm his shields and shut down his engines."

"Wouldn't that affect you in the same way?" Folan asked.

"Not if we're not here." Picard rose and pivoted to Spock. "In your report you said Folan found that the zone around the sphere was not normal space—point 'a' didn't lead to point 'b.' "

"It must," Spock said, "but not in the way in which we can perceive it."

Picard considered that a moment. "If we thrust ourselves into the zone around the sphere, we may appear where? Data?"

"Difficult to predict, sir. We will not know how well we can navigate until we test the modifications to the sensors' algorithms."

"But we'll have to enter that area no matter what?"

"Yes, Captain."

"How much time do we have, Spock?" Picard was formulating a plan. For the first time in days he felt a cohesive idea forming and he was enjoying the sensation after so much meandering and guesswork. He had Riker, Data, Troi, and Spock all back. T'sart and Lotre were under control, and Kalor was recovering. The only missing element was Parl and his ship. They should have ventured into the system by now.

"We cannot know at what rate the dead zones are expanding," Spock told Picard, "but I can tell you the disruption in this system alone is increasing at a rate of six percent every hour."

"No time to waste." Picard made his decision. "Number One, I want to beam one of our shuttle's warp cores directly into space. Ten thousand kilometers off this Medric's bow. Right between us."

"Aye, sir." Riker nodded and buried himself in his console.

The captain came up behind the helm and rested his hands on the conn chair's headrest. "Rossi, lay in a course, full impulse, right toward the sphere."

"That won't be the course we'll end up on," Folan said. Picard looked back at her. She was holding her shoulders as if cold. He had to admire her bravery, standing up to all the powers of her oaths and people, and disregarding them to trust those of an "enemy" government.

"I'm counting on it," he told her, and tried to give a slight inspirational smile.

They saw the white bubble in space, then felt the shock wave of the matter-antimatter explosion—but only for a moment. Then it was in the distance. Then halfway close again, and then—they didn't know where.

The whining was back—the distortion and audio howl that had plagued them when they'd only dipped a toe into the zone near the sphere. It was somewhat better, but not by much.

"Mr. Spock, I take it this is as much protection as the shields will afford us?"

"I'm afraid so, sir," Spock said.

"I'm generating a low warp field for some extra protection, but it won't last long, Captain," La Forge added.

"Then we'd better hurry," Picard said. "Can we navigate?"

"I can't make heads or tails, sir—it's—" Suddenly Rossi cried out in pain.

Picard rushed toward her, grabbing the woman as she fainted and collapsed into his arms.

"Data, take the helm," he ordered. "Riker, take her."

The captain handed Rossi off to his first officer, who jabbed at his combadge. "Riker to sickbay."

There was no response.

"Internal comms are down, sir," Chamberlain advised.

"Confirmed," La Forge said. "I just lost contact with engineering. I need to head down there. I'll take her to sickbay on my way."

The captain nodded to Riker. "Help him, then coordinate all decks to use computer access for communication. Readouts only."

"Aye, sir," Riker said as he and La Forge took Rossi and quickly escaped into a turbolift.

As Picard turned, the unignorable hum of the spatial distortion around him grating his nerves, Data called for his attention.

"Captain, I—I seem to be able to understand this readout."

Picard's eyes went wide. He'd never heard incredulity from the android's voice, even with his emotion chip. "Data?"

Spock rose and glided to the helm. "Fascinating."

"You can plot a course?" Picard asked.

Data nodded. "I believe so, sir."

"Captain, I regret I didn't consider this possibility sooner."

Another shock, first Data, now Spock, saying the most unexpected things. "Explain."

"Mr. Data is not bound by our natural predilection to a four-dimensional perception."

Picard sighed and rubbed his temples with his fingertips. "Explain again, Mr. Spock."

At the helm, Data's hands were now flying over the console. His expression was as a child's on Christmas morning having found his favorite toy under the tree. "I was not even aware I had this ability."

"Until now, you may not have," Spock told him, then turned back to Picard. "There was never a frame of perception under which it could develop. Humanoids are unable to perceive more than the common four dimensions, length, width, height, and time. But *mathematically* we postulate higher dimensions. Commander Data is a being of mathematical precision—"

"Thank you, sir," Data said.

Spock continued. "He is not bound by our more limited, biological perceptions."

Picard nodded and turned to pace toward the upper deck and back. "The Edo . . . a culture with whom we came into contact soon after the *Enterprise*-D was commissioned. They had a—what they called a god, but was some sort of higher-dimensional group of beings. Their vessel was in space, and also not."

"In space, and in unperceived space," Folan corrected, drawing Picard's attention and stopping him in his gait.

"Yes," he nodded his acceptance of his mistake.

"Sir, I have a course," Data reported.

They all looked to him, then to the helm console and the gibberish which infested it.

The captain motioned for Spock and Folan to take seats, and he took to his command chair as well.

"Mr. Data," he said. "Engage."

Chapter Nineteen

Chapter Nineteen

REALITY MELTED, CONGEALING INTO GLOBS of matter that bounced and bubbled and mocked Picard's senses. He looked across the bridge and space itself seemed to poke through the bulkheads around the edges of the main viewer.

Spock was saying something but it was distorted. Everything was deformed and twisted. Data's head turned toward the captain—or maybe just space did, and Data did nothing himself to cause that appearance.

Noise without tone crushed down on them. Picard covered his ears, but this was no vibration that rode the air. There was nothing to keep out, as the sound was the vibration of everything—without and within.

He was screaming in pain now, or so he thought—it wasn't as if he heard his own voice. He heard everything else, everywhere, his perception told him.

Picard fell back into his command chair, and then down onto the deck. He forced himself to focus, not on his perceptions, but on raw thought. What was happening? He needed to reason it out and concentrate on that.

Higher-dimensional—"Aaarggh!"

He couldn't think—the pain was too much. He just wanted it to end—life itself, if not the agony.

And then, it did—the agony, at least. It was as if he'd been wired to an electric chair and someone finally cut the power. Exhausted, aching, and sore, Picard struggled to pull himself into the command chair again. His eyes slowly opened, and Spock stood before him.

"Are you all right, Captain?" The Vulcan offered him a helping hand.

Gladly, he accepted it and rose to his feet. "I think so, Mr. Spock. Are you?"

Looking no different than fifteen minutes before, Spock said, "I am recovering."

Picard moved toward the helm, limping a bit. "Data?"

The android turned back to him, the oddest, most satisfied smile on his face. "We are inside the sphere, sir."

The captain spun to look at the forward viewer. "Inside . . ." Picard breathed, taking in the vast starscape across it. He moved to the ops panel and punched up a few different sensor views, looking port, then starboard, then aft. "There's only space outside. What's happened to the sphere? What have we managed to do?"

"I believe, sir, what we're seeing is a graphical representation, but I cannot be sure." Data rose from the helm and strode up to the science station. Spock and

Picard followed. Folan still seemed to be recovering in her chair before the console.

"Graphical? A representation of what?" Picard asked.

"This star system." Data checked one readout, then another, and another. "Sensors are functioning completely now, sir. Distortions continue outside, but we are not affected. We are, however, able to scan outside. Apparently, the interior is a gigantic astrometrics projection system, though I do not detect any such technology at play."

The captain shook his head, awed. "Data, how did you manage it?"

"I am unable to explain it, sir," the android admitted. "To me, the path seemed relatively clear."

Picard leaned down to him, placing a hand on Data's shoulder. "What did it look like to you?"

Brows swung upward innocently, Data shook his head. "I do not think I can accurately describe it, sir. It was . . . more, is the best way to explain it."

"More what, Data?"

"More space, sir."

Picard thought about that, and struggled to remember elementary physics discussions about higher dimensions: how a theoretical two-dimensional man would be imprisoned within a circle the same way a 3D man would be so entrapped by a sealed cube. A 3D man would not be ensnared by a circle—because he had the luxury of more space. He could step over the same prison walls a 2D man could not.

"You're right," Picard said with a sigh. "I don't understand. At least not so much I can picture it, but I do grasp the theoretical concept." He looked to the forward screen again and the clear view of the system across it. There, in the distance, was the Caltiskan sun, kept from being sucked into the black hole near it for uncounted millennia by an ancient science. Picard assumed that, had he ordered magnification, he would have seen Medric's ship, disabled and drifting.

"Are you *sure* we're inside?" he asked.

"We can say little with complete certainty," Spock said. "But it would seem that within this device is 'the eye of the storm' in a sense."

Picard's headache pounded not very lightly behind his eyes. "What is this . . . device supposed to do?"

Coming from seemingly nowhere, a bright, intrusive light filled the bridge. Both Data and Spock turned to the sensors as the captain looked at Chamberlain and made sure the lieutenant was ready for a possible attack.

"Captain, we are being scanned," Data reported. "Very active, very intrusive."

"Intrusive?" Chamberlain asked, glaring at his tactical board. "It's like someone walked in on the ship while in the shower."

Spock nodded. "This scan is occurring on all degrees, including sub-quantum levels."

It was Folan's turn to look surprised. "Someone is scanning us below the quark plane?"

"That is correct, Sub-Commander. Very sophisticated," Spock commented. "We are barely able to register it."

"Where is it coming from?" Picard demanded, stalking the science station consoles.

"From the sphere itself, I imagine," Spock replied. "I

cannot get a fix. These sensors are primitive in comparison."

Primitive. The word conjured ox carts and oil lamps, not isolinear sensors and deflective scanners.

Picard asked again in frustration, chastising no one in particular, "What is this device supposed to do?"

A klaxon sounded.

"Intruder alert," Chamberlain said. "I think."

"You think?" In a moment, Picard was at the tactical board next to the young lieutenant.

"Something's breaking through our shields like they weren't there, sir."

The captain motioned to Spock and Data. "Scan that. But I don't want to stop it."

"Sir?" Chamberlain looked aghast. "You're going to let them—"

"Whoever they are," Picard said, "assuming there's an intelligence here and not merely an automated process, could have destroyed us by now easily with the power at their discretion."

Solidifying onto the bridge in a flash of light and slight buzz of energy, a computer console materialized between the conn and ops control boards.

Picard approached the addition, which looked strikingly like any other *Enterprise* control kiosk. "Data?"

The android was already running a tricorder over the console. Spock was likely scanning it as well from the science station.

"It is not our equipment," Data commented.

His lips pursed, Picard nodded. "I gathered that."

"No, sir, I mean to say, internally this is not our technology. I cannot ascertain any standard technological references."

"But it looks like one of your consoles," Folan said, approaching it cautiously.

Data closed his tricorder and holstered it. "As an interface, yes. I believe it has been put here for our convenience, designed to look and act as our own equipment."

Nodding his agreement, but continuing to poke at the science station controls, Spock weighed in. "The sphere has apparently scanned us and created a console for our use."

Picard motioned for Data to investigate it, and as he did, the captain watched anxiously over his shoulder. It did look and act like a normal control pad, but the information on it was flowing so quickly only Data, and perhaps Spock, could have understood it.

"Sir," Data began cautiously, "I believe that this sphere is not attempting to disrupt the surrounding space. In my estimation, it is attempting to scan it."

"Scan it?" Picard felt his brow furrow and he leaned down as if examining the console closer would help. "Are you sure, Data?"

"I am sure," Spock replied, rising from his station and making his way to the lower deck of the bridge. "As Commander Data suggested, the dynamics of this console, while obviously made to fit into your ship's systems, are far more advanced than our technology. That said, its processes are clear. It is scanning the universe. A scan so strong, it exceeds the quantum level and touches the very fabric of reality itself. And in doing so, disrupts it."

Picard would be fascinated if there were time. "But can you stop it from scanning and disrupting space?"

Data shook his head. "Sir, I believe this console is only for information-gathering purposes and has no command interface. There is, however, evidence of a vocal link to whatever the console is connected to."

Picard nodded, jumping on the chance to issue some orders. "Computer tie-in to alien console between conn and ops stations."

A flurry of bleeps and beeps as the *Enterprise* computer tried to do so, melding its circuits with complex alien technology.

"Link complete," the familiar *Enterprise* computer voice reported. And then the alien console spoke in a deeper tone: "DIMENSIONAL SCANS PROCEEDING."

Hesitating only a moment, Picard cocked his head to one side and stared at the console as if it were a person standing before him. "What . . ." he began, and paused again, searching for the right question. He must start, he thought, at the beginning. "What are you?"

"I AM A VEHICLE."

"A vehicle?" Spock asked.

"CORRECT."

"It said dimensional scans," Folan whispered, then turned to Picard. "Perhaps it scans all dimensions, then is able to traverse them with ease?"

"It has a very disruptive way of doing it," Picard said tightly.

"Other dimensions?" Chamberlain asked. "As in subspace?"

Spock turned to the tactical officer. "Not quite. The primary Unified Field Theory has suggested that the universe is ten-dimensional in nature."

"Yes, yes, we studied that," Picard remembered. "With all ten dimensions stable at the time just before the Big Bang, when the universe was a mass of matter/energy."

The Vulcan nodded. "Indeed. And the Big Bang itself was the collapse of that monobloc."

Chamberlain was barely looking at his console now. He was caught up in the discussion, the predicament. "Don't you mean explosion?"

"Yes, and no," Spock replied. "Dimensionally, it is believed to be the point at which the six higher space-time dimensions collapsed, leaving the four in which we exist to be the most accessible."

"But this sphere is accessing them," Picard said, making a gesture that included the device in which they rested.

"So have we," Folan said, nodding to her own internal understanding. "At least to differing degrees of success—and at the expense of great power. And if nothing else, we know this sphere is controlling immense energies." She turned to Spock. "There are Romulan theories along these lines as well. They suggest that when the universe has expanded past a certain point, the force of gravity will pull all matter and energy together again, into the monobloc of matter/energy you spoke of. In that monobloc, the ten dimensions of space-time are again full, but unstable, creating another Big Bang, and another universe."

"All fascinating," Picard interrupted, "but our galaxy—"

"Universe, sir," Data corrected, still tapping commands into the alien kiosk to view information. "I believe the dimensional scans are being conducted universe-wide."

Picard motioned widely, his hands tight fists. "Very well. All the more urgent. Our universe is *dying*. How do we stop it?"

Data shook his head, softly shrugging. "There is no data on that from this console, sir."

"Computer tie-in to the alien console," Picard ordered again, then spoke directly to the sphere. "Dimensional vehicle, can you discontinue the spatial disruptions in the universe outside?"

"AFFIRMATIVE."

"Then please do so," Picard asked, "immediately!"

The alien computer was silent, but space outside was changed.

Chapter Twenty

"WHAT'S HAPPENING?" PICARD DEMANDED.

"I AM FOLLOWING THE ISSUED COMMAND," replied the alien console, and Picard felt a small degree of panic rise in his chest. Something was wrong. Nothing good was this easy. He pivoted toward the rear of the bridge.

"Spock?"

The Vulcan and Data had transferred the alien kiosk's output to the science stations.

After a moment, Spock turned back the captain, his face a Vulcan pale-green almost yellow ashen. "Space-time, the universe, is now in a state of hypercontraction," Spock said, his tone dire. "Uncounted times faster than the speed of light, and infinitely faster than space-time would in the normal life of the universe, all existence is collapsing in on itself. Galaxy after galaxy, empty void after empty void." What he said next made it Picard's unspoken fault. "The source of contraction is the sphere."

"What?" Folan seemed to wince, her face crumpled, looking ill. "What is happening?"

Spock flicked a switch on his console, and the forward viewscreen flashed with a magnified view of the dark side of the Caltiskan planet. Lights, the signs of civilization seen from orbit, went dark all over the planet.

"A dead zone," Picard said, his voice sounding hollow.

"I believe," Data explained, "the universe is quickly and prematurely returning to the state it would after billions and billions of years of life—the monobloc of matter/energy of which you recently spoke. The precursor to this is one final, massive dead zone."

"Why is it not affecting us?" Picard asked. But the answer was obvious.

"I surmise the sphere is immune."

"You're saying," Picard said, "the sphere is not a part of the universe?"

Spock swiveled easily around in his seat. "The universe, defined as all that which exists, necessitates that it *is*. However, it must exist on a level outside the impact of that which goes on around it."

"How is that possible?" Folan asked the question Picard was thinking.

The Vulcan shook his head. "We do not know."

The words pinched at Picard, biting into him. "I'm hearing a lot of that. We need to understand this!"

"Captain, the science at this level borders on magic to our understanding," Spock's voice was apologetic, smooth, but laced with just a hint of concern. If he and Data truly didn't know . . .

Picard rubbed the back of his neck and the knot that wouldn't go away. "Moses would have thought a light bulb was magic, Mr. Spock, but given enough time, I'm sure it could have been explained to him."

"Of that I have no doubt," Spock replied. "But someone would need to be able to explain the technology. I cannot."

"What *can* you explain?" he snapped.

"Little. But I do now believe this device is an artifact from a Type IV civilization."

Picard squinted at him, remembering yet another theory—this one taught in high school rather than the Academy. "I've heard of types one through three, I believe . . ."

"I've not," Folan said, running a hand through her hair.

Spock made sure to turn so he could address both her and Picard. "A long-standing theory of technological advancement, not as measured by specific inventions, but in use of energy. A Type I civilization would be able to control the energy of its own planet. Twenty-first-century Earth was such a civilization."

"Yes, I remember this," Picard said, nodding. "A Type II civilization would be like our own—a culture which can control the energy of entire solar systems."

"Correct, and a Type III civilization controls the power and energy of an entire galaxy," Spock said.

"As I remember, that's where the theory ended— with a Type III civilization." Picard felt they shouldn't be discussing this so calmly, but he needed to understand the problem to form a solution, if there was one.

"I believe it is time to revise that theory," Spock offered. "It is possible the sphere and its makers, were, or are, from a Type IV civilization—with the ability to harness and manipulate the power and energy of the universe itself."

Data, still watching the torrent of information that flowed from the alien kiosk as it transferred to his science station, voiced his own hypothesis. "Captain, in my estimation, the purpose of this machine, this vessel, is for interdimensional travel. It exists not only in the four dimensions in which we live, but the six higher dimensions that make up the complete fabric of the universe."

"That would explain why there is more area *inside* than outside the sphere. Inside the sphere is higher-dimensional space," Picard suggested.

Correcting that notion, Spock shook his head. " 'Inside' may be as inaccurate a concept here as 'up' and 'down' are in the space we routinely traverse. But, if the race that created the sphere became a Type III civilization, and could travel time in this universe, then they had an infinite amount of time to bring themselves to Type IV."

Struggling to sort the possibilities, Picard gnashed his teeth at the swirl of information that contradicted most physics he knew—and yet supported it as well. "So, the purpose of this vessel is to travel both time and space? The *Enterprise* can do that."

"This object has survived from within a black hole," Spock said, "and is unaffected by the universe outside. Most likely it will be able to survive the monobloc that will quickly follow the collapse of this universe."

Picard marched down toward the alien console. "Is this correct?"

"PARTIALLY."

It was coming together in Picard's mind. He saw the path being laid. "You'll . . . use the energy from the end of the universe itself to propel yourself into the next universe?"

"SIMPLISTIC, BUT NOT INACCURATE," replied the console's deep baritone.

"Captain, if I may, this computer is not unlike the being-computer on the Guardian planet."

Spock's comment made something click in the back of Picard's mind, and he remembered the Guardian planet and its portal across time and space.

"Yes, we're familiar with that planet. Are you suggesting the same race created this?"

The Vulcan shook his dark head. "The interface is different, so I would not venture a guess, but one would think they are at least similar in the level of their technology. Perhaps both Type IV civilizations."

"The 'next universe' . . ." Picard whispered, his gaze intent on the alien computer monitor.

"An interesting concept," Folan murmured, perhaps equally awed by the posibilities. "And a confusing one," she added.

"Remember that existence is a constant that cannot be broken." Spock steepled his fingers and seemed to address all on the bridge. "Existence exists. It simply *is*. This is the base metaphysical axiom inherent in all facts of reality. While the nature and shape of the universe is perhaps cyclical—from monobloc, to Big

Bang, to expansion, then collapse, and then monobloc again, forever—the existence of the base matter/energy is inescapable."

"The oscillating universe theory." Picard nodded as he lowered himself into the command chair and gazed at the stars on the main viewer. "The universe changes, blanking out all matter every time it reverts to a monobloc . . . but existence remains, and the sphere can traverse the monobloc, using the power of the end of the universe itself as a boost."

Spock raised a brow. "Yes, that is my supposition. Well stated. And apparently that is the operation now in effect."

"Stop this process," Picard ordered.

Neither defiant nor apologetic, the alien kiosk replied. "I CANNOT."

"You must!" Picard pounded his fist on the arm of his chair.

"Captain, it is a machine." Suddenly Spock was at his side. "As such, it can only act as it was programmed."

"Pardon me, sir," Data interjected from the rear of the bridge, his voice just a touch insulted.

"Present company excluded, Commander," Spock apologized.

"Thank you, sir."

"Of what use is a piece of technology that can go to the next universe only by destroying the one it is in?" Picard demanded.

The sphere itself answered: "I AM ABLE TO MOVE TO THE END OF THE UNIVERSE, OR BRING THE END ABOUT. EITHER METHOD IS AVAILABLE."

A chill ran down Picard's spine. He'd done this. He'd given the sphere an order, and brought about the destruction of everything. In his haste to save lives, he'd ended them—all.

What could they now do? "Spock, if the sphere can move forward to the end of the universe, then perhaps it could go back and allow us to stop this at the beginning?"

"THAT METHOD OF TRAVEL IS UNAVAILABLE." Unfeeling, uncaring words.

"Apparently not," Spock said.

"Then . . . *we're* all saved," Picard said heavily, "and everyone else is dead."

"Captain, if nothing else, this is a fantastic opportunity for scientific discovery—the end of the universe." Data had not moved from his console in some time, nor had he looked up. "The sphere has enhanced our sensors. We can draw information on any star in any galaxy . . . we're watching it happen."

"We've *caused* it, Data!" Picard barked. "We need a way to stop it, not study it!"

Hands clasped thoughtfully behind his back, Spock's soft voice seemed more for his own ears than for anyone else's. "We may not be able to stop it in this universe, but surely these events will take place again."

Picard looked up at him. "Pardon?"

Spock lowered himself into the seat next to the command chair. "Assuming that this cycle of existence is infinite, since matter/energy cannot be destroyed, there is a statistical certainty that all that has happened in this incarnation of the universe will occur again, in a proceeding incarnation."

Closing his eyes, the captain shook his weary head and tried to grasp what Spock was telling him. "Explain."

"As far as we know matter and energy can neither be created nor destroyed—simply changed from one into the other. Matter/energy is what the universe is constructed of. With only a finite number of ways which it might form such constructs, and yet an infinite number of chances to attempt them . . . think of it like this. You have a pile of bricks. There are a limited number of ways you might stack them to build a house, and yet with unlimited attempts, you will at some point repeat the way in which you stack the bricks. Given that, these circumstances must happen again—as well as any other possible circumstances—an infinite number of times, in an infinite number of proceeding universe incarnations."

The captain nodded. "Parallel universes. Statistically, since there are finite combinations in which particles can react physically, there will be infinite such universes as ours. A former crewmate of ours had some hard experience with that theory—he went from parallel universe to parallel universe until he was finally able to find his way home."

Spock nodded. "As have I. How often these alternative time tracks will appear is another matter. There could be, and most likely would be, trillions upon trillions of 'universes' completely unlike our own before one would be similar enough that the same events would occur."

Silently, Picard looked at the alien computer console a long moment, then asked the question he'd only now considered. "In how many other universes will I make this same mistake?"

"An infinite number," Spock replied.

"So not only have I destroyed this universe, but others." The captain's voice was bitter, and he didn't mind if his crew knew it. His crew—they went about their jobs, La Forge still working in engineering, Riker coordinating damage control on various decks, Crusher treating wounded . . . life went on for them. And outside . . . outside the sphere it did not.

"If I may, sir," Spock said, "those would be other Picards, in other universes."

Finally risen from his seat at the science station, Data stepped down to the lower bridge. "With respect, Ambassador, we cannot be assured of that. I have been studying the data from the alien console and a fear has been realized. The dimensional scans that have been taking place were not merely universe-wide, but existence-wide. All universes, preceding and proceeding, were being examined by the sphere. By ending those processes prematurely, we may have hastened the end of not merely our universe, but all of them.

"Existence itself is being reset. Within their respective time periods, all universes will revert to monoblocs, essentially rebooting every universe and starting it over."

"Every universe?" Picard shook his head, not wanting to believe it. "All of them?"

"At least those I have been able to scan, sir."

Picard marveled at the thought: All that had happened in his universe would eventually play out again in some other universe, and perhaps in an infinite number of others as long as matter/energy existed.

More riveting still was the notion that other Picards would make the same mistake he had—his fate was not only to take the blame for ending his own universe, but infinite others.

"How could I have done this?" Mouth agape, the captain of the *Enterprise* grappled with the concept of not something as simple as the death of himself, his crew, his ship, or a planet, a people, a race, or even a galaxy, or a universe . . . no, those were all too small to describe the burden on his shoulders. He'd decided the fate of the universe, and in doing so, ended it for untold numbers of beings across time.

He couldn't let it end, not all things, everywhere. He couldn't let infinite universes die as he survived. "There must be a way to undo this," Picard almost growled. "A process is taking place—it can be stopped." Rising, he looked at Spock and Data and even Folan, and pointed to the alien kiosk in the center of his bridge. "Find it."

Chapter Twenty-one

U.S.S. Enterprise, NCC 1701-E
Romulan space
Caltiskan system

Now

THERE ARE THOSE IN SOME CULTURES who sit in prison cells and await their own deaths as decreed by law, sometimes for just reasons, and sometimes not. When not, their burden must be heavy and ponderous, suffocating and overwhelming. Such was Picard's now. Not because he awaited his own end, but because he awaited the end of every being he could imagine, and an infinite number he could not.

Pulling the captain's thoughts back to the bridge, Data tapped Picard's shoulder. "Captain? We know more now."

Only allowing himself the slightest scrap of hope, Picard looked up from his command chair. "Tell me we can stop this, Data."

The android nodded. "Yes, sir. Ambassador Spock and I believe the process *can* be stopped from within the sphere, but because this sphere is the source of the problem, our galaxy may be sacrificed nonetheless. The hyperaccelerated contraction of the 'Big Crunch' has begun."

Pushing himself up, Picard gripped Data's shoulders. "But the universe, and all reality will be safe?"

Nodding as if Picard had asked if they were still serving prime rib in the mess hall, Data replied, "We believe so, sir."

What had he done? How had the death of an entire galaxy become a beacon of hope in Picard's mind?

Tense, all his muscles taut with both hope and horror, Picard demanded to know how. "What must we do?"

Spock stepped forward from the science station. "We need to initiate an end to the sphere itself, Captain. By sending the sphere prematurely into its journey to the next incarnation of the universe, before the 'Big Crunch' has completed, it will lack the power necessary to survive the voyage. It will no longer be able to complete the hypercontraction it's begun."

"What about galaxies already destroyed?" Picard demanded. "What about other changes? Are you telling me no one will notice the universe has been moved a little to the right?"

"No galaxies have yet been destroyed," Spock explained. "However it is likely the dead zones have permeated it completely by now."

"So, what about us?" Chamberlain asked.

Making a half turn to him, Spock replied. "With the sphere gone, *Enterprise* will be in her own galaxy again . . . in the center of a large dead zone."

Out of even her scientific league, Folan had long ago relegated herself to the seat next to Picard's command chair. She spoke up now, her voice weak with fatigue. "But we could stay where we are, could we not? If we do nothing, we merely watch the birth of a new universe?"

"Yes," Data said. "But the old one would still die."

"Everyone will be dead," Folan said. "Everyone we knew—"

"Everyone in our galaxy," Data said. "But not everyone in our universe."

His chest heavy, a sorrowful pressure gripping his heart, Picard knew what he must do. His only regret was that the solution had been found too late to help his own galaxy and the trillions upon trillions who would die without power. His life was forfeit, perhaps with his galaxy's, but in that act he might save the bulk of existence itself.

"Make it so."

U.S.S. Enterprise, NCC 1701-D
Romulan space
Caltiskan system

Now

"What about us?" Tasha Yar asked.

Angling toward her, Spock replied. "With the

sphere gone, the *Enterprise* will be in her own galaxy again, and we will perish in the massive power desert."

Out of even his scientific league, T'sart had long ago relegated himself to the seat next to Picard's command chair. He spoke up now, his voice weak from exhaustion. "We could stay where we are, however? If we simply do not act, will we not see the birth of a new universe?"

"Yes," Spock replied. "But the current one would nevertheless perish."

"Everyone is dead," T'sart lamented. "My wife . . . my family . . ."

"Yes, perhaps they are," Picard admitted, raking his fingers through his wet mop of hair. "But others in our universe, and countless others, are not."

Captain John L. Picard would not allow the destruction of existence to rest on his shoulders. He was a hero, and he would be to the end.

"Mr. Spock, do it."

U.S.S. *Constitution*, NCC-41869
Federated Worlds space
Caltiskan system

Now

"What about us?" Tobin asked.

Swinging on his heel, Lore replied. "With the sphere gone, we'll be in our galaxy again." The android shook his head. "Sadly, we'll all perish in the dead zone that remains."

Worf, son of Ja'rod, pounded at his tactical board. "This is insanity! We could stay where we are and live forever! Captain, I implore you, do not make this choice. All we know is already lifeless."

"Yes, it is," Picard barked. "But others in our universe, and countless others, are not."

Captain Robert Picard of the *U.S.S. Constitution* would not allow the destruction of existence to rest on his shoulders. He would not be remembered as the man who destroyed the universe.

"Mr. Lore, do what we must."

U.S.S. Enterprise, NCC 1701-E
Romulan space
Caltiskan system

Now

"Spock? Data?" Picard turned toward them, Folan close at his side. "Nothing happened." On the forward viewer, the Caltiskan star shone brightly, the black hole opposite it still a dark cavity in space.

"Something *has* happened, Captain," Spock reported, bent over the scanners. "The sphere is gone."

"And," Data added, "there seems to be no sign the sphere was here." He glanced back to where the kiosk had been. "None at all."

"Captain," Chamberlain called excitedly. "Multiphasic transmissions on all subspace bands! Starfleet, sir! I can hear Starfleet!"

"The dead zones? Gone?" Picard looked to Data.

"Apparently, sir."

"A dream?" Folan asked, touching her face to see if she was still alive. "Is this all a dream?" She chuckled nervously.

She was losing herself, Picard thought. He took her by the shoulders and shook her once. "Sub-Commander, listen. Listen!"

"What?" she said. "This is all insane!"

He set her down in the command chair and marched to Spock and Data. "Confirm and explain," he ordered.

"I cannot," Spock said, "except to suggest that my calculations were too limited. I assumed you'd be acting alone. Statistically I should have known I was mistaken."

"Whom else was I acting with, Mr. Spock?" Picard demanded. "I did think I was the only one here."

"Here, indeed. But not now."

The captain crossed his arms. "Mr. Spock, speak plainly."

Spock looked to Data, giving Picard the annoying impression that they'd decided the android was more used to explaining the more difficult scientific concepts to Picard and so should take the lead.

"Yes, by all means, Mr. Data," Picard said sarcastically. "Do help your addle-minded captain."

"Of course, sir," Data deadpanned. "While you

acted to save existence at the loss of our galaxy, another Captain Picard, or other-named counterpart, under similar circumstances did the same. At the loss of his galaxy, he acted to save our universe."

"Of course," the captain whispered.

"I don't understand," Folan murmured. "This makes no sense. We were supposed to die."

"We did not," Data said matter-of-factly. "In an infinite number of both preceding and proceeding incarnations of the universe, Captain, the same brave act saved every other universe. Every Picard's loss was negated by all the others."

"I'd considered," Spock said, "but not included in probability outcomes, this very important piece of the puzzle—that these same events were taking place in similar universes throughout existence."

A regretful cast to his expression, Data said, "I did not think of it either, sir. But I concur that the existence of an infinite number of situations like this, with your counterparts all acting similarly, changed the outcome for all the others. Including ourselves."

Feeling an odd mix of relief and foolishness, Picard slumped against one of the guard rails that separated the command deck from the upper bridge. "I just barely saved all I knew . . . and I can't even claim I did that alone."

Spock nodded. "I cannot help but agree. But if I may, Captain, you have also saved *more* than you knew. Unlike any Starfleet vessel before us, we have learned that existence is not finite, but a constant . . . and expansive . . . and still mostly unknown."

"Truly," Picard murmured, "the final frontier."

"No," Spock said, drawing Picard with his voice to glance up and see the slightest smile tug at the Vulcan's lips. "If there is one thing we have learned, it is that nothing is final."

Epilogue

U.S.S. Exeter, NCC-26531
Alpha Quadrant unexplored sector
Section 3

Now

THEY'D SHUT DOWN THE BRIDGE days ago—or maybe it was weeks—and now Captain James Venes's command consisted of sickbay, engineering, two cargo bays, and the few corridors and hatchways that connected them. The crew had food rations to last, and plenty of water, but it was heat and light he most worried about.

That, and the boredom, Venes thought as he rubbed an irritation from his eye. Morale was low . . . hundreds of people waiting to die, their ship already a mostly cold husk. Batteries for life-support would only last another few days. He knew it . . . and so did they. The captain was supposed to go down with his ship—the crew was not.

Chemical thrusters had served only to get them nowhere slowly, and they had burned out days ago. Escape pods, useless for extended travel as there was nowhere to go, had been cannibalized for battery packs and foodstuffs.

All that done, what was left to them? Counting the hours.

Venes had thought of everything he could . . . and it wasn't enough. So it felt as if he'd done nothing—a thought he'd probably take to his grave.

And then the lights flashed on. He looked one way, then another as power thrummed within the veins of the starship, up the bulkheads, and through to her soul. People stood slowly, in awe of their vessel around them, squinting into the new light. Venes reached for his combadge and had to strain to hear his chief engineer—the crew in the cargo bay, and throughout the ship, were cheering.

"Alvaro?"

"I have no idea why, sir."

"Everything's back?" Venes stepped into the corridor, unsure of exactly where he was going.

"Full power is available," Ortiz said, chuckling with incredulity and glee.

The captain shook his head, smiled, and marched forward with renewed purpose. "Get the rest of the ship back online and have the senior officers meet me on the bridge."

"*Aye, sir.*"

"Good work, Mr. Ortiz," Venes said.

"*Yes, sir. Not mine, but maybe someone's.*"

U.S.S. Voyager, NCC-74656
Unexplored sector
Delta Quadrant

Now

"Captain?" B'Elanna Torres pulled herself from under the access panel and stared up at the warp core as it seemed to awaken itself. She scurried over to one of the status consoles.

"I see it," Janeway said.

Thirty hours of battery power had been stretched, painfully, into five days. And now, just as the ship was growing cold, as the air was running out . . .

"We're back?" Torres saw the power levels, not just creeping up on all screens, but leaping up.

"We're back!" Janeway said.

From a computer station toward the doors that opened into the corridor, Seven of Nine looked at Chakotay next to her, then Janeway. "So are the Borg. I hear them."

The captain nodded and strode toward the door. "Alert the crew," she ordered Chakotay. "Get the bridge back online, as well as the Doctor." She shook her head ruefully. What had kept them trapped with the Borg ship could also be their doom if they didn't warm their engines before their enemy warmed their own. "As soon as we can, have Paris get us out of here. Maximum warp." Treading up the already warming corridor, Janeway thought to herself that they'd cheated death again, and could continue their voyage home.

Klingon Warship *Qulric*
Romulan space
Caltiskan system

Now

"Sir, it is definitely a dead zone. There is no escape." The *Qulric* science officer offered Parl a padd of data.

Angrily, Parl waved it away. "There must be an escape! Picard has not reported back—we *must* help him."

Governor Kalor was on *Enterprise*. His oldest friend, his blood brother . . . he could not be dead. He *must* not be dead. Parl would not let that happen. They'd been at each other's weddings, seen each other's children grow and become warriors . . . and seen their home colony destroyed at the hands of T'sart's evil spatial traps. Parl had felt enough loss, and would tolerate no more.

"I don't care what it takes," he said. "I don't care who I must kill, but I want this ship at full power! Now!"

And so they did. Instantly. Parl wheeled toward the viewscreen, ordering it on. Shimmering to view, a picturesque starscape—no more spatial distortion—and in the distance, *Enterprise*.

"Can we hail them?" Parl pivoted toward the communications officer.

"We can hail anyone, sir," the man said, tapping at his console. "We have full subspace communications. I am reading Romulan, Federation Starfleet, Klingon Defense Force Command, and civilian channels, all open and very active."

Parl nodded once. "Hail the *Enterprise,*" he said, and lowered himself in the command chair.

"They are hailing us, sir. Governor Kalor wishes to speak with you."

Pushing out a relieved sigh, Parl motioned for the connection to be put on the main viewer. "It would seem the galaxy is waking from its sleep."

Three weeks later

Familiar sand crunching under his feet, Deanna on his arm, Riker thought he'd never see Folan again, let alone the street beneath him. "I must say I'm impressed. Treaty notwithstanding, I wouldn't have thought this visit politically possible."

The Romulan commander nodded. "For some it is a new era, Mr. Riker."

"And for you?" Deanna asked, squinting slightly in the bright evening sun as it angled over the trees.

"Things are . . ." Folan hesitated, and Riker wondered if she was uncomfortable with the changes in her life, such as the new rank, or simply was uncomfortable as to how much she should say. "Things are going well," she said finally.

"There have been rumors about T'sart." Riker kicked a stone along the path and watched it skitter up the walk.

Folan nodded, and not dispassionately. She wanted to talk about this. "As you know, most of the major Alpha Quadrant governments have vied for his extradition. But now the matter is moot," she paused dramatically. "The transport that was taking him from the homeworld to the penal holding colony . . . inexplicably exploded soon after leaving port." She smiled, just a touch. "Of course, a full investigation has begun."

"Of course," Riker said. "And someday it might even complete."

The Romulan woman lowered her eyes in acceptance. "Perhaps."

As they opened the gate before them, Deanna asked, "And the Caltiskans?"

"Their system is safe, once again," Folan said. The last to step through the yard's small gate, she closed it behind them all. "The technology that allows their star and planet to not be torn into the black hole is unchanged, and again under their care. We are in negotiations regarding reparations for their civic and population losses."

Deanna nodded approvingly. "And Tobin?"

At the mention of his name, Folan seemed to shrug. "He is welcome to stay with you. The terms of the treaty are such that one cannot 'defect' as such. He may return to Romulus should he wish it. Should you speak with him, you may tell him he's been decorated with the highest civilian honor for bravery."

Riker chuckled. "I'm sure he'll be pleased."

Just as they reached the door, Folan put a hand on his arm and drew his attention. "And tell your . . . tell Picard he should have been granted one as well."

"You have my word on it," Riker said, and smiled warmly.

"Well, someone should ring the bell." Deanna looked for a button to push on the side of the door.

Riker made a fist and wrapped on the door. "This'll do."

A few moments' wait, and Nien was opening the door. She saw first Deanna, then Riker, and was obviously stunned with delight. "Oh . . . my . . . Ri-ker . . ." Then she noticed Folan and a look of worry creased her face. "Who are you?"

"Commander Folan, ma'am," she said softly. "Jolan true to you."

Still a quick detector of good character, Nien opened her door widely and smiled. "Jolan true. Please come in." She gestured for them to enter, then looked up at Riker. "I didn't think to see you again."

Riker reached down and kissed her hand. "Hey, someone buys me, they buy the best." With his other hand he reached into his tunic pocket and pulled out a small bag. "I couldn't let you give your life savings for our cause and see nothing in return." He pressed the bag into her hands.

She opened it, slowly, old fingers fumbling with the tie. "Latinum?" she asked with a gasp. "This is far more than—"

"Courtesy of Starfleet."

"And," Folan added, "I hear from someone with Senate influence that your husband's pension has been increased."

With sparkling eyes that seemed to know all, Nien

winked at her fellow Romulan. "Someone of influence, eh?" She set the bag of latinum on the table next to her and closed her front door. "Can you all stay for dinner?"

Riker threw up his hands in surrender. "How can I resist an evening with three charming and beautiful ladies?"

"You cannot," Nien said, glowing with delight. "Just one thing, child." She patted him on the arm and drew them all into her home. "I'll do the cooking."

"People like us, who believe in physics, know that the distinction between past, present, and future is only a stubbornly persistent illusion."

—ALBERT EINSTEIN

ACKNOWLEDGMENTS

As always there are people to thank when a task such as this is finally complete. These are the people who collectively make it difficult for me to be anything but humble when someone tells me they enjoyed *my* book. It's never just Greg's and mine—not when so many other people put their time and effort into seeing the project through to publication.

Since I'm the one writing the acknowledgments, I'll start by thanking the other guy whose name goes on these books. Greg Brodeur provides most of the plot and a lot of the characterization of what you read. He chips away at what shouldn't be in a chapter, and lets me know what should be in one. Despite all that, I assure you anything you didn't like is his fault, and anything you loved was my idea. That said, I will be tearing this page out of his copies of this book. I'll send him a thank-you card and tell him I skipped acknowledgments this time. So this is all between us, right?

A hearty thanks must go to Keith R. A. DeCandido. His eye for detail and overall creative touch was much appreciated and needed. And boy does he know his *Trek!* Thanks, Keith.

It goes without saying that I thank John J. Ordover,

Trek Senior Editor and head honcho supreme. A more reasonable and tolerant editor there never was.

My thanks also to Josh Lothridge, a "starving" writer himself, who not only was quick with needed research, but pretty good on picking out an awkward phrase and rubbing my nose in it the way only a twerpy little brother can. Thanks, Josh.

Of course, thanks also to the many friends and family who understood there were occasions I was too busy working on these books to hang out with them: my parents, Diane, Lydia, Gordon and Ben, Alvaro, Steve, Pino, Lyn, Len and Wendy, my cousins, Peg and Larry, and all my ComicBoards.com buds who wondered why I wasn't on-line as much.

One last thank-you to those of you who E-mailed me feedback on our last book, *Battle Lines*. Whether people enjoyed it or not, they took the time to let me know, and that's always a good thing. Okay, it was better when they enjoyed it, but I'll take the bad with the good. Seriously, thanks for keeping in touch.

Cheers,
Dave Galanter
DaveGalanter@aol.com
www.comicboards.com/dave

Look for STAR TREK fiction from Pocket Books

Star Trek®: The Original Series

Star Trek: The Next Generation®

Star Trek: Deep Space Nine®

Star Trek: Voyager®

Star Trek®: New Frontier

Star Trek®: Invasion!

Star Trek®: Day of Honor

#1 • *Ancient Blood* • Diane Carey
#2 • *Armageddon Sky* • L.A. Graf
#3 • *Her Klingon Soul* • Michael Jan Friedman
#4 • *Treaty's Law* • Dean Wesley Smith & Kristine Kathryn Rusch
The Television Episode • Michael Jan Friedman
Day of Honor Omnibus • various

Star Trek®: The Captain's Table

#1 • *War Dragons* • L.A. Graf
#2 • *Dujonian's Hoard* • Michael Jan Friedman
#3 • *The Mist* • Dean Wesley Smith & Kristine Kathryn Rusch
#4 • *Fire Ship* • Diane Carey
#5 • *Once Burned* • Peter David
#6 • *Where Sea Meets Sky* • Jerry Oltion
The Captain's Table Omnibus • various

Star Trek®: The Dominion War

#1 • *Behind Enemy Lines* • John Vornholt
#2 • *Call to Arms...* • Diane Carey
#3 • *Tunnel Through the Stars* • John Vornholt
#4 • *...Sacrifice of Angels* • Diane Carey

Star Trek®: The Badlands

#1 • Susan Wright
#2 • Susan Wright

Star Trek®: Dark Passions

#1 • Susan Wright
#2 • Susan Wright

Star Trek® Books available in Trade Paperback

Omnibus Editions
    Invasion! Omnibus • various
    Day of Honor Omnibus • various
    The Captain's Table Omnibus • various
    Star Trek: Odyssey • William Shatner with Judith and Garfield Reeves-
      Stevens

Other Books

STAR TREK®

STICKER
BOOK

MICHAEL OKUDA
DENISE OKUDA
DOUG DREXLER

POCKET BOOKS
A VIACOM COMPANY

STAR TREK

isbn: 0-671-01472-2

STKR

STAR TREK
SECTION 31

BASHIR
Never heard of it.

SLOAN
We keep a low profile....
We search out and identify
potential dangers to the
Federation.

BASHIR
And Starfleet sanctions
what you're doing?

SLOAN
We're an autonomous
department.

BASHIR
Authorized by whom?

SLOAN
Section Thirty-One was
part of the original
Starfleet Charter.

BASHIR
That was two hundred years
ago. Are you telling me
you've been on your own
ever since? Without specific
orders? Accountable to
nobody but yourselves?

SLOAN
You make it sound so
ominous.

BASHIR
Isn't it?

No law. No conscience. No stopping them.
A four book, all _Star Trek_ series beginning in June.

Excerpt adapted from _Star Trek:Deep Space Nine_®
"Inquisition" written by Bradley Thompson & David Weddle.

2161

From John Vornholt
author of *Gemworld*

STAR TREK

THE NEXT GENERATION®

GENESIS WAVE

Book Two of Two

Based on the long-hidden scientific secrets of
Dr. Carol Marcus, who has mysteriously
disappeared, the dreaded Genesis Wave is
sweeping across the Alpha Quadrant, transforming
entire planets on a molecular level and threatening
entire civilizations with extinction.

The finest engineers of three civilizations,
including Geordi La Forge and his long-lost love,
Dr. Leah Brahms, must race against time to devise
some way of halting the deadly wave before
yet another world can be transformed into
something entirely alien and unrecognizable.

But even if the Genesis Wave can be defeated,
Picard must still confront the greater mystery of
what unknown intelligence dared to launch the
wave against an unsuspecting galaxy—and for
what malevolent purpose....

Coming in hardcover from

Pocket Books
A VIACOM COMPANY